"You'd like me to r

column from the

***the* Courier?"**

"What?"

"Maybe it will jog your memory if I tell you that the headline is 'The Sheikh and the Chauffeur'? Or do you want all the gory details of how Sheikh Zahir al-Khatib was seen gazing into the eyes of his pretty chauffeur as he waltzed her around Berkeley Square at midnight?"

"How on earth—?"

"For heaven's sake, everyone with a camera phone is an amateur paparazzo these days, Di! Even if the snapper didn't recognize Sheikh Zahir, a man dancing with his chauffeur made it a story. The fact that he looks lost to the world makes it the kind of story that the *Courier* was always going to run in its diary column. I don't imagine it took them more than two minutes to identify Sheikh Zahir. He's not exactly a stranger to the gossip pages."

"He isn't?"

"He's a billionaire bachelor, Diana, what do you think?"

Think?

Who was thinking?

"Oh…"

Dear Reader,

My first book, *An Image of You,* was published fifteen years ago, and I still remember the rush of excitement, the thrill of receiving a phone call to say that this publisher, who had been part of my reading life for so long, wanted to publish my book.

This year I will be writing my fiftieth Harlequin Romance®, and the thrill remains.

Love truly is the most powerful human emotion, and there is nothing more rewarding than writing—and reading—a story that reveals the strength, tenderness and unique capacity for sacrifice of the human heart.

In *The Sheikh's Unsuitable Bride,* Diana Metcalfe lives in a small, terraced house in London, while jet-setting sheikh Zahir al-Khatib lives in luxury in an exotic and beautiful palace. Yet it is not the vast social gulf that divides them, but the demands of family and duty that seem destined to keep them apart. Only love can find a way....

With warmest wishes,

Liz

LIZ FIELDING
The Sheikh's Unsuitable Bride

DESERT BRIDES

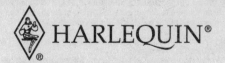

HARLEQUIN®

TORONTO • NEW YORK • LONDON
AMSTERDAM • PARIS • SYDNEY • HAMBURG
STOCKHOLM • ATHENS • TOKYO • MILAN • MADRID
PRAGUE • WARSAW • BUDAPEST • AUCKLAND

ISBN-13: 978-0-373-18345-6
ISBN-10:   0-373-18345-3

THE SHEIKH'S UNSUITABLE BRIDE

First North American Publication 2008.

www.eHarlequin.com

Printed in U.S.A.

DESERT BRIDES

When an ordinary girl meets a sheikh...

*If you love reading stories set in distant, exotic lands
where women just like you are swept off their feet
by mysterious, gorgeous desert princes—
then you'll love this miniseries!*

*Look out for more DESERT BRIDES stories
coming soon from Harlequin Romance®.*

If you want to escape the winter and jet off to the
intense, balmy heat of the desert—then make a date
with Barbara McMahon next month!

RESCUED BY THE SHEIKH

When photographer Lisa Sullinger gets stuck
in the desert, the last thing she expects is to be
rescued by a sheikh! Lisa can't help but fall for
brooding Tuareg al Shaldor.... Is there a place for
a small-town girl like her in his guarded heart?

Liz Fielding started writing at the age of twelve, when she won a writing competition at school. After that early success there was quite a gap—during which she was busy working in Africa and the Middle East, getting married and having children—before her first book was published in 1992. Now readers worldwide fall in love with her irresistible heroes, and adore her independent-minded heroines. Visit Liz's Web site for news and extracts of upcoming books at www.lizfielding.com.

Don't miss Liz's next book

THE BRIDE'S BABY

Part of the sparkling *A Bride for all Seasons* mini-series

Out in April, only from Harlequin Romance®.

CHAPTER ONE

'LEAVE that, Di.'

Diana Metcalfe backed out of the rear door of the minibus she was cleaning and, stuffing a handful of chocolate wrappers into her overall pocket, turned to face her boss. The woman, unusually, looked as if she was just about at the end of her tether.

'What's up, Sadie?'

'Jack Lumley has gone home sick. He's the third today.'

'The café's meat pie strikes again?'

'So it would appear, although that's the Environmental Health Officer's problem. Mine is that I've got three drivers with their heads down the toilet and a VIP with a packed schedule arriving at London City Airport in a little over an hour.' Despite her worries, she managed a wry smile. 'Please tell me you don't have a hot date tonight.'

'Not even a lukewarm one.' Who had the time? 'You want me to work this evening?'

'If you can.'

'It shouldn't be a problem. I'll have to give Dad a call, let him know he'll have to give Freddy his tea.'

'How is your gorgeous little boy?'

'Growing like a weed.'

'Daisy keeps asking me when he can come over for another play-date.' Then, 'I'll fix up something when I call your father. You don't have time, not if you're going to meet that flight.'

Diana blinked. Meet the flight...? 'Excuse me? Are you saying that I get the VIP?'

'You get the VIP.'

'But I can't! You can't...'

Sadie frowned. 'You've been checked out on the car haven't you?'

'Um, yes...' Company rules. Everyone could, in theory, drive any car, in the Capitol fleet. In theory. But this was the newest, most luxurious, most *expensive* saloon car in the garage—pride and joy of Jack Lumley, the company's number one driver. While she'd anticipated a shuffle round to take up the slack, an extra job or two, never, in her wildest dreams, had she imagined she'd ever be entrusted behind its leather-covered steering wheel.

Or entrusted with one of their top drawer clients.

'Thank goodness for that,' Sadie said with feeling.

Apparently, she could!

Diana slapped a hand over her mouth, but not quickly enough to catch the word that slipped out.

Sadie sighed. 'Please tell me you don't use that kind of language when you're on the school run, Diana.'

'Me? Oh, please! Where on earth do you think I learned a word like that?'

'Are the kids really that bad? My father took it on as a public service, something for the local community, but I won't have—'

'The kids are okay,' she said quickly. 'Really. They're just at that age where shocking the grown-ups is a sport. The trick is not to react.'

'The trick, Di, is not to join in.'

'I don't…' Realising that she just had, she let it go. 'Right.'

Sadie looked thoughtful. 'I've half a mind to put Jack on the job for a week or two when he's fit. Teach them to think twice about their language. Teach him to think twice about eating dodgy meat pies on my time.'

The senior driver of Capitol Cars reduced to driving a minibus full of lippy primary school kids?

Having swiftly recovered from her shock, Diana grinned. 'Now that's something I'd pay good money to see.'

They exchanged a glance. Two single mothers— one at the bottom, the other at the top of a male-dominated business—who between them had heard every chauvinist put-down, every woman driver joke in the book. Sadie, with obvious regret, shook her head. 'Unfortunately he'd resign rather than do that.'

'Totally beneath his dignity,' Diana agreed. 'I'm sure learning that I've been driving his precious car will be punishment enough.'

Sadie just about managed to stop herself from grinning back and snapping back into 'boss' mode she said, 'Yes, well, just remember that at this end of the business the clients prefer their chauffeurs politely invisible.'

'No singing, then?'

'Singing?'

'I find it keeps the passengers from using bad language...'

'I'm serious!'

'Yes, ma'am.'

'Right. Well, come on. I'll brief you on Sheikh Zahir's itinerary while you change. This is a full dress uniform job. And yes, before you ask, that includes the hat.'

'Sh...Sh-Sheikh?'

Diana thought she'd managed to cover her near slip pretty well, but Sadie's quick glance suggested that she was not fooled.

'Sheikh Zahir al-Khatib is the nephew of the Emir of Ramal Hamrah, cousin of his country's ambassador to London and a billionaire businessman who is single-handedly turning his country into the next *über*-fashionable get-away-from-it-all tourist destination.'

Diana instantly lost any inclination to sing. 'He's a genuine A-list VIP, then.'

'You've got it. The Mercedes is at his disposal full-time while he's in London. The hours will, inevitably, be unpredictable but if you can hold the fort for me today, I'll have someone else lined up to take over tomorrow.'

'You don't have to do that,' Diana said a touch fiercely, hoping to counteract the initial impression of irresponsibility. She might not be Jack Lumley, but her passengers were never short-changed. 'I can handle it. At least until Jack has recovered.'

This was the chance she'd been waiting for, an opportunity to prove herself capable of taking on the big jobs, to move up from the no-frills end of the market—the school bus, the airport runs—to driving one of Capitol's limousines and big money; she wasn't about to meekly surrender the Mercedes to the first man to recover control of his stomach.

'Give me a chance, Sadie. I won't let you down.'

Sadie touched her shoulder, a gesture that said she understood. 'Let's see how it goes today, shall we?'

Okay. She got the message. This was her opportunity to show what she could do; it was up to her to make the most of it.

Diana responded to the challenge by peeling off

the latex gloves she used for cleaning out the minibus with a decisive snap. Then she stepped out of her garage overalls and replaced them with well-pressed trousers, a fresh white shirt and, instead of her usual Capitol Cars sweatshirt, her rarely worn burgundy uniform jacket.

Sadie, consulting a sheet on the clipboard she was holding, said, 'Sheikh Zahir is flying into the City Airport in his private jet, ETA seventeen-fifteen hours. Wait in the short-term parking area. The VIP hostess has the number of the car phone and she'll give you a call when his plane touches down so that you can be at the kerb, waiting for him.'

'Got it.'

'His first stop will be his country's embassy in Belgravia. He'll be there for an hour, then you're to take him to his hotel in Park Lane before leaving at nineteen-forty-five hours for a reception at the Riverside Gallery on the South Bank, followed by dinner in Mayfair. All the addresses are on the worksheet.'

'Belgravia, Mayfair...' Diana, unable to help herself, grinned as she buttoned up her jacket. 'Be still my beating heart. Is this a dream? Should I pinch myself?'

'Don't go all starry-eyed on me, Di. And keep in touch, okay? Any problems, I want to hear about them from you, not the client.'

* * *

Sheikh Zahir bin Ali al-Khatib was still working as the jet touched down and taxied to the terminal.

'We've arrived, Zahir.' James Pierce removed the laptop, passed it on to a secretary to deal with, and replaced it with a gift-wrapped package.

Zahir frowned, trying to recall what it was. Then, remembering, he looked up. 'You managed to find exactly what she wanted?' he demanded.

'One of my staff located it via the Internet. Antique. Venetian. Very pretty. I'm sure the princess will be delighted.' Then, 'Your usual driver will be waiting at Arrivals but we've a very tight schedule this evening. You'll need to leave the embassy no later than eighteen-forty-five hours if you're going to make the reception on time.'

Diana pulled up at Arrivals, squashed the stupid little forage hat firmly into place, tugged down her uniform jacket, smoothed the fine leather gloves over the backs of her hands. Then, her head full of snowy robes, the whole Lawrence of Arabia thing, she stood by the rear door of the limousine, ready to leap into action the minute her passenger appeared.

There were no robes. No romantic headdress caught by the wind.

Sheikh Zahir al-Khatib had, it seemed, taken on board the dressing-for-comfort-when-travelling message. Not that she'd have had any trouble recognising him, even without his VIP escort.

The grey sweatshirt, soft jeans and deck shoes worn on bare feet might be casual but they were expensive. The man, tall and rangy, with dark hair that curled around his neck, might look more like a sports star than a tycoon, but his clothes, his head turning looks, did absolutely nothing to diminish an aura of careless arrogance, the aristocratic assurance of a man whose every wish had been someone else's instant command from the day he had first drawn breath.

The very pink, thoroughly beribboned gift-wrapped package he was carrying provided no more than a counterpoint that underlined his authority—the kind of presence that raised the hairs on the back of her neck.

Sheikh Zahir al-Khatib, it had to be admitted, was dangerously, slay-'em-in-the aisles, gorgeous.

He paused briefly in the doorway to thank his escort, giving Diana a moment to haul her chin off the ground—drooling was such a bad look—before affixing a polite smile to lips that she firmly compressed to contain the usual, 'Did you have a good flight?' chat as she opened the rear door of the car.

No chat.

This wasn't a family party returning from a trip

to Disney, eager to share their good time as they piled into the minibus, she reminded herself.

All that was required was a quiet, Good afternoon, sir…

It wasn't easy. There were two things she was good at: driving and talking. They both came as naturally to her as breathing: one—just about—paid the bills, the other she did for free. Sort of like a hobby. A fact that had featured prominently in her end of year school reports.

Talking in class. Talking in Assembly. Talking herself into trouble.

Since she mostly got the kids and the hen parties—jobs where a bit of lip came in handy if things got rowdy—it wasn't usually a problem, but she understood why Sadie would only give her a job like this if she were really desperate.

Why she'd reserved judgement on anything more than a fill-in role.

Well she would show Sadie. She would show them all, she promised herself—her parents, that older generation of neighbours who gave her that no-better-than-she-should-be *look*—and she began tidily enough.

Her smile was regulation polite as she opened the door smartly so that nothing would impede his progress.

'Good afternoon—'

She didn't get as far as the 'sir'.

A small boy, skidding through the terminal doors in her passenger's wake, dived through the closing gap between the car door and Sheikh Zahir, to hurl himself at the woman who'd just pulled up behind them. Before Diana could utter a warning or move, he went flying over her highly polished shoes and cannoned headlong into Sheikh Zahir, sending the fancy package flying.

The Sheikh's reactions were lightning-fast and he caught the child by the back of his jacket before he hit the ground.

Diana, no slouch herself, leapt for the ribbons.

The package was arcing away from her, but those ribbons had their uses and she managed to grab one, bringing it to a halt.

'Yes!' she exclaimed triumphantly.

Too soon.

'No-o-o-o!'

She held the ribbon, but the parcel kept travelling as the bow unravelled in a long pink stream until the gift hit the concrete with what sounded horribly like breaking glass.

At which point she let slip the word she'd promised Sadie that she would never, ever use in front of a client.

Maybe—please—Sheikh   Zahir's   English wouldn't be good enough to grasp her meaning.

'Hey! Where's the fire?' he asked the boy, hauling

him upright and setting him on his feet, holding him steady while he regained his balance, his breath, and completely dashing her hopes on the language front.

Only the slightest accent suggested that the Sheikh's first language wasn't English.

'I am so-o-o-o sorry…' The boy's grandmother, the focus of his sprint, was overcome with embarrassment. 'Please let me pay for any damage.'

'It is nothing,' Sheikh Zahir replied, dismissing her concern with a graceful gesture, the slightest of bows. The desert prince to his fingertips, even without the trappings.

He was, Diana had to admit, as she picked up the remains of whatever was in the parcel, a class act.

Then, as she stood up, he turned to her and everything went rapidly downhill as she got the full close-up impact of his olive-skinned, dark-eyed masculinity. The kind that could lay you out with a smile.

Except that Sheikh Zahir wasn't smiling, but looking down at her with dark, shaded, unreadable eyes.

It was only when she tried to speak that she realised she'd been holding her breath.

'I'm sorry,' she finally managed, her words escaping in a breathy rush.

'Sorry?'

For her language lapse. For not making a better job of fielding the package.

Deciding that the latter would be safer, she offered it to him.

'I'm afraid it's broken.' Then, as he took it from her and shook it, she added, 'In fact it, um, appears to be leaking.'

He glanced down, presumably to confirm this, then, holding it at arm's length to avoid the drips, he looked around, presumably hoping for a litter bin in which to discard it. Giving her a moment to deal with the breathing problem.

So he was a sheikh. So his features had a raw, dangerous, bad boy edge to them. So he was *gorgeous*.

So what?

She didn't do that!

Besides which, he wasn't going to look at her twice even if she wanted him to. Which she didn't. Really.

One dangerous-looking man in a lifetime was more than enough trouble.

Definitely time to haul her tongue back into line and act like the professional she'd promised Sadie she was...

There wasn't a bin and the Sheikh dealt with the problem by returning the sorry mess of damp paper and ribbons to her. That at least was totally masculine behaviour—leaving someone else to deal with the mess...

'You're not my usual driver,' he said.

'No, sir,' she said. He had twenty-twenty vision, she thought as she retrieved a waterproof sick bag from the glove box and stowed the package inside it where it could do no harm. 'I wonder what gave me away?' she muttered under her breath.

'The beard?' he offered, as she turned to face him.

And his hearing was…A1.

Oh, double…sheikh!

'It can't be that, sir,' she said, hoping that the instruction to her brain for a polite smile had reached her face; the one saying, Shut up! had apparently got lost *en route*. 'I don't have a beard.' Then, prompted by some inner demon, she added, 'I could wear a false one.'

Sometimes, when you'd talked your way into trouble, the only way out was to keep talking. She hadn't entirely wasted her time at school. She knew that if she could make him laugh, she might just get away with it.

Smile, damn you, smile…

'If it's essential,' she added, heart sinking. Because he didn't.

Or comment on what was, or was not, essential.

'What is your name?' he asked.

'Oh, you needn't worry about that,' she assured him, affecting an airy carelessness. 'The office will know who I am.'

When he made his complaint.

She wasn't even going to last out the day. Sadie would kill her. Sadie had every right…

'Your office might,' he said, 'but I don't.'

Busted. This was a man who left nothing to chance.

'Metcalfe, sir.'

'Metcalfe.' He looked as if he might have something to say about that, but must have thought better of it because he let it go. 'Well, Metcalfe, shall we make a move? Time is short and now we're going to have to make a detour unless the birthday girl is to be disappointed.'

'Birthday girl?'

Didn't he know that it was seriously unPC to refer to a woman as a 'girl' these days?

'Princess Ameerah, my cousin's daughter, is ten years old today. Her heart's desire, apparently, is for a glass snow globe. I promised her she would have one.'

'Oh.' A *little* girl… Then, forgetting that she was supposed to only speak when she was spoken to, 'They are lovely. I've still got one that I was given when I was…'

She stopped. Why on earth would he care?

'When you were?'

'Um, six.'

'I see.' He looked at her as if trying to imagine her as a child. Apparently failing, he said, 'This one was old too. An antique, in fact. Venetian glass.'

'For a ten-year-old?' The words were out before she could stop them. On the point of stepping into the car, he paused and frowned. 'I mean, *glass*. Was that wise?' She had the feeling that no one had ever questioned his judgement before and, trying to salvage something, she said, 'Mine is made from some sort of polymer resin.' It had come from a stall at the local market. 'Not precious…' except to her '…but it would have, um, bounced.'

Shut up now!

Her shoulders lifted in the smallest of shrugs, disassociating the rest of her from her mouth.

'Since it's for a child, maybe something less, um, *fragile* might be more sensible. Glass is a bit, well…'

Her mouth finally got the message and stopped moving.

'Fragile?' Sheikh Zahir, still not smiling, finished the sentence for her.

'I'm sure the one you bought was very beautiful,' she said quickly, not wanting him to think she was criticising. She was in enough trouble already. 'But I'm guessing you don't have children of your own.'

'Or I'd know better?'

'Mmm,' she said through closed lips. 'I mean, it would have to be kept out of reach, wouldn't it?' She attempted a smile to soften the message. 'It is… was… a treasure, rather than a toy.'

'I see.'

He might be dressed in the most casual clothes, but there was nothing casual about his expression. He was still frowning, although not in a bad way, more as if he was catching up with reality.

Face aching with the effort of maintaining the smile, Diana ploughed desperately on. 'No doubt princesses are less clumsy than ordinary little girls.'

'Not,' he said, taking her breath away for the second time as he finally responded to her smile with a wry contraction of the lines fanning out from his charcoal eyes, 'in my experience.' Nowhere near a slay-'em-in-the-aisles smile, but a heart-stopper none-the-less. At least if her heart was anything to go by. 'You're not just a pretty face, are you, Metcalfe?'

'Um…'

'So, how much would it take to part you from this hard-wearing toy?'

She swallowed. 'I'm sorry, but I don't have it now.'

His brows rose slightly.

'It didn't break,' she assured him. 'I gave it to…'

Tell him.

Tell him you gave it to your five-year-old son.

It was what people did—talk incessantly about their kids. Their cute ways. The clever things they did.

Everyone except Miss Motormouth herself; how ironic was that?

She'd talk about anything except Freddy. Because when she talked about her little boy she knew, just

*knew, that all the listener really wanted to know
was the one thing she'd never told a living soul.*

Sheikh Zahir was waiting. 'I gave it to a little boy
who fell in love with it.'

'Don't look so tragic, Metcalfe, I wasn't serious,'
he said, his smile deepening as he mistook her reluctance to speak for an apology. 'Let's go shopping.'

'Y-yes, sir.' Then, with a glance towards the terminal
building, 'Don't you want to wait for your luggage?'

She'd assumed that some minion, left to unload
it, would appear at any moment with a laden trolley
but, without looking back as he finally stepped into
the car, Sheikh Zahir said, 'It will be dealt with.'

Sadie was right, she thought. This was another
world. She closed the door, stowed the remains of
the precious glass object out of harm's way and
took a deep breath before she slid behind the wheel
and started the engine.

Shopping. With a sheikh.

Unbelievable.

Unbelievable.

All James's careful planning—every second ac-
counted for—brought to naught in an instant of
distraction.

But what a distraction…

Zahir had walked through the arrivals hall expecting the efficient and monosyllabic Jack Lumley

to be waiting for him. Instead he'd got 'Metcalfe'. A woman whose curves were only emphasized by the severe cut of her jacket. A woman with a long slender neck, against which soft tendrils of chestnut hair were, even now, gradually unfurling.

And a mouth made for trouble.

The kind of distraction he didn't have time for on this trip.

No complaints. He loved the excitement, the buzz of making things happen, didn't begrudge a single one of the long hours it had taken to turn a small, going-nowhere company running tours into the desert into a billion dollar business.

He'd single-handedly taken tourism in Ramal Hamrah out of the stopover business—little more than a place for long-haul passengers to break their journey to shop for gold in the souk, take a sand dune safari—into a real industry. His country was now regularly featured in travel magazines, weekend newspaper supplements—a destination in its own right. Not just for the desert, but the mountains, the history.

He'd created a luxurious tented resort in the desert. The marina complex was nearing completion. And now he was on the point of launching an airline that would bear his country's name.

He'd had to work hard to make that happen.

Until he'd got a grip on it, tourism had been considered little more than a sideshow alongside the oil industry. Only a few people had had the vision to see what it could become, which meant that neighbouring countries were already light years ahead of them.

Perhaps it was as well; unable to challenge the dominance of states quicker off the starting blocks, he'd been forced to think laterally, take a different path. Instead of high-rise apartments and hotels, he'd gone for low impact development using local materials and the traditional styles of building to create an air of luxury—something entirely different to tempt the jaded traveller.

Using the desert as an environmental spectacle, travelling on horseback and camel train, rather than as a rip-'em-up playground for sand-surfers and dune-racers. Re-opening long-ignored archaeological sites to attract a different kind of visitor fascinated by the rich history of the area.

And a change of attitude to international tourism in the last year or so had given him an edge in the market; suddenly he was the visionary, out in front.

Out in front and on his own.

'...you don't have children of your own...'

Well, when you were building an empire, something had to give. A situation that his mother was doing her best to change. Even as he sat in the back of this limousine, watching Metcalfe's glossy chestnut hair unravel, she was sifting through the likely applicants for the vacant post of Mother-Of-His-Sons, eager to negotiate a marriage settlement with the lucky girl's family.

Make his father happy with the gift of a grandson who would bear his name.

It was the way it had been done for a thousand years. In his culture there was no concept of romantic love as there was in the West; marriage was a contract, something to be arranged for the mutual benefit of two families. His wife would be a woman he could respect. She would run his home, bear his children—sons who would bring him honour, daughters who would bring him joy.

His gaze was drawn back to the young woman sitting in front of him, the soft curve of her cheek glimpsed in the reflection of the driving mirror. The suggestion of a dimple.

She had the kind of face that would always be on the point of a smile, he suspected, smiling himself as he reran the range of her expressions—everything from horror as she'd let slip a word that was definitely not in the Polite Chauffeur's Handbook, through blushing confusion, in-your-face take-it-or-leave-it cheek and finally, touchingly, concern.

Glass. For a child. What on earth had he been thinking? What had James been thinking?

That was the point. They hadn't been. He'd just ordered the most expensive, the most desirable version of the child's wish and James had, as always, delivered.

A wife wouldn't have made that mistake.

Metcalfe wouldn't have made that mistake.

Nor would she settle for a relationship based on respect, he suspected. Not with that smile. But then she came from a different world. Lived a life unknown to the young virgins from among whom his mother would look for a suitable bride.

Very different from the sophisticated high-achieving career women who he met in the line of business, who lived their lives more like men than women, although what she lacked in gloss, sophistication, she more than made up for in entertainment value.

He dragged his fingers through his hair, as if to erase the unsettling thoughts. He didn't have time for 'entertainment'. And, with marriage very much on the agenda, he shouldn't even be thinking about it.

As it was, he had to snatch this hour to celebrate a little girl's birthday out of a crammed schedule when he should, instead, be concentrating on the reception for travel journalists and dinner with the men who had the financial power to make his airline a reality.

'Are you a permanent fixture, Metcalfe?' he asked. 'Or will Jack Lumley be back on duty tomorrow?'

'I couldn't say, sir,' she said, glancing up to look in the rear-view mirror, briefly meeting his gaze, before returning her attention to the road. 'He was taken ill earlier today.' Then, 'I'm sure the company could find you someone else in the meantime, if you insisted.'

'Someone with a beard?'

'Yes, sir.'

Her dimple had disappeared. She wasn't smiling now. Not even close. She thought he objected to a female chauffeur?

'And if I did?' something made him persist. 'What would you be doing tomorrow?'

Her eyes flickered back to him. They were green, like the smudge of new leaves in an English hedgerow in April.

'If I'm lucky I'll be back at the wheel of a minibus, doing the school run.'

'And if you're unlucky?'

'Back at the wheel of a minibus, doing the school run,' she repeated, letting loose another of those smiles, albeit a somewhat wry one, as she pulled into the forecourt of a massive toy store. She slid from behind the wheel but he was out of the car before she could open the door for him and looking up at the façade of the store she'd chosen.

It hadn't occurred to him to dictate their destination. Jack Lumley would have taken him to Harrods or Hamleys, having called ahead to check which of them had what he was looking for, ensuring that it would be gift-wrapped and waiting for him, charged to his account.

No waiting.

No effort.

Like an arranged marriage.

A gust of wind whipped across the vast forecourt of the store and Diana grabbed for her hat, clutching it to her head.

Sheikh Zahir had made no move to enter, but was staring up at the storefront and, heart sinking, she realised that she'd got it wrong.

Sadie was right. She wasn't equipped for this…

'I'm sorry,' she said. 'This isn't what you expected.'

He glanced back at her. 'I left the decision to you.'

True. And she'd made her best judgement…

'I thought it would be quicker,' she explained. 'It's certainly easier to park.' Then, 'And, to be honest, you don't quite meet the Knightsbridge dress code.'

'There's a dress code?' He turned to look at her. 'For *shopping?*'

'No bare feet. No sports shoes. No jeans. No backpacks.' She faltered, realising just how foolish she must sound. As if anyone would turn *him* away for being inappropriately dressed. 'Not that you're carrying a backpack.'

'But I tick all the rest of your boxes.'

'I expect it's different for royalty.'

'Just as well not to risk it,' Sheikh Zahir said gently. If he was laughing at her, he was being kind enough not to do it out loud.

On the point of congratulating herself that she wasn't such a juggins after all, he said, 'Okay. Let's do this.'

Let's. As in 'let us'. We.

'You want me to come in with you?'

'Surely you were told that royalty never carries its own bags?'

Now she was quite sure he was laughing.

'The rumour is that they don't carry money either and you should know that I can't help you there.' Then, 'Besides, I really shouldn't leave the car.'

'Are you refusing to come with me?' he enquired, a faint edge beneath the chocolate silk of his unbelievably sexy accent. A reminder that she was there at his bidding. 'The school run is that appealing?'

Maybe she'd been too quick to leap to judgement on the 'kind', she decided, locking the door and following him without another word.

Inside a store of aircraft hangar proportions, aisle upon aisle of shelves were stocked with everything a child—and quite a few grown-ups—could possibly desire.

Diana found herself staring at the shopping trolleys, the serve-yourself warehouse-style shelving, not through her own eyes, but through the eyes of a man for whom 'self-service' was undoubtedly an un-explored concept.

It was most definitely another one of those 'oh, sheikh' moments.

'So much for this being quicker,' he said, looking around. 'How on earth do you find what you're looking for?'

'With difficulty,' she admitted, realising that at one of those Top People's stores, someone would have found exactly what he was looking for in an instant. 'The, um, idea is to get you to pass as many shelves as possible. That way you're more likely to impulse buy.' Then, 'How many people, do you suppose, leave with the one item they came in to buy?'

He turned to look at her. 'That sounds like the voice of experience.'

'Isn't that what I'm here for? My experience? You're the one who bought something made of glass for a little girl.'

'Actually…' He stopped, shook his head. 'I take your point, although I'm now beginning to think I'd be better advised to buy Ameerah shares in the company.'

'Shares in a toy shop?' she said, clutching her hands to her heart. 'Now why didn't my parents think of that?'

'Because they're not so much fun to play with, I

imagine,' he said seriously. 'Not what a little girl imagines for her birthday surprise.'

'True, but just think what I could do with them now.' His brows rose slightly, inviting an explanation. 'Instead of the five-minute gratification of a plastic car for my favourite doll, I could now afford to buy my own taxi. Be my own boss.' Then, because his eyebrows lifted another millimetre, 'I'd go for the fun version in sparkly pink, obviously…'

CHAPTER TWO

ZAHIR watched as Metcalfe swiftly turned and walked across to the enquiry desk, jolted out of his preconceived notion of who she was, what she was.

Not just an attractive young woman at the wheel of a car, but an attractive young woman with aspirations, dreams.

Not so long ago, he'd been there.

People assumed that because he had been born the grandson of the Emir of Ramal Hamrah life had fallen into his lap. Maybe they had a point. He'd been indulged, he knew that, with every benefit that life could bestow, including a privileged education in England, the freedom of post-graduate studies in America. But there was a price to pay.

Duty to his country, obedience to the family.

He'd spent two years in the desert, with his own life on hold, as companion to his grieving cousin. His reward had come when Hanif, seeing that his heart lay not with the slow-grinding wheels of government, but in the fast-moving world of big business, had given him his first chance. Had given his own precious time to convince his father that he should be allowed to tread his own path.

Had taken time to explain that what he was doing was as important for his country as playing the diplomat, the courtier, particularly when he would be such a reluctant one.

Even so, he'd had to go to the market for the money he'd needed to build his empire from the ground up, but, while his name could not guarantee success, he knew it had opened doors for him. People had been polite, inclined to listen, because of who he was, whereas even now he could see that his chauffeur was getting the most grudging attention from the assistant at the desk.

'Do they have what we're looking for?' he asked, joining her.

'Who knows?'

As she went to ask for help from an assistant, Diana was desperately wishing she'd gone for the obvious shopping destination instead of trying to be clever. In Knightsbridge she would have had to stay with the car to fend off the traffic warden while he 'shopped' all by himself.

'If they have any they'll be with the novelty items.' Her imitation of the assistant's couldn't-be-bothered gesture, made without looking up from whatever she was finding so gripping in the magazine she was reading, was meant to be ironic. 'Over there, apparently.'

Maybe Sheikh Zahir didn't 'get' irony because he turned to the woman behind the desk and said, 'We don't have a great deal of time...' he paused to check out her name tag '...Liza. Would you be kind enough to show us exactly where we can find what we're looking for?'

She turned a page and said, 'Sorry. I can't leave my desk.'

Big mistake that, Diana thought, warmed by his 'we'.

'I can't', as she'd already discovered for herself, did not impress him one bit.

'The sign above your desk says "Customer Service",' he pointed out and then, as she sighed and finally looked up, he smiled at her.

Diana watched, torn between outrage and amusement as, without another word, the assistant leapt to her feet and scurried round the desk.

'This way,' she said, switching on a smile of her own. One of the hundred watt variety.

'We seem to have beaten the system, Metcalfe,' Sheikh Zahir said as, with a gesture, he invited her to follow the woman.

'Nice work,' she said, 'but somehow I don't think that technique would work for me.'

That earned her a smile of her own. Rather less than he had used on the assistant, but at the same time more, she thought.

Less teeth. More eyes.

'You use what you have,' he said with a shrug.

Fortunately, before she was called upon to reply, they arrived at a shelf lined with a colourful selection of snow globes.

'Cinderella. Snow White. The Princess and the Frog.' The assistant, her attention now fully engaged by Sheikh Zahir, indicated the range on display. She couldn't have been more enthusiastic if she'd made each one personally. By hand.

'Thank you,' Sheikh Zahir said as he picked up the Princess and the Frog.

'If there's anything else…?' she offered, lingering, transformed by his smile into a candidate for Customer Services Assistant of the Year award.

'I'll be sure to come and find you.'

It was polite, but there was no doubt about it. She'd been dismissed. Diana almost felt sorry for her as she backed away, dragging her tongue after her. Almost.

'The Princess and the Frog, Metcalfe?' he asked, holding out the globe for an explanation.

He had beautiful hands. Not pampered or soft. There was an old scar running across his knuckles and, although his fingers were long, thin even, it was the slenderness of tensile steel.

'I am not familiar with this fairy tale,' he said.

'I'm surprised you know any of them,' she said, forcing herself to focus on the globe. It contained a scene in which a girl, wearing a small crown, and a frog were sitting on the edge of a well.

'Disney has reached Ramal Hamrah.'

'Has it?' Of course it had. 'Oh, right. Well, I suppose this must be one he decided to give a miss.' She thought about it. 'Actually, he was probably right. I'd stick with one of the others,' she advised.

'But this girl is a princess. Ameerah will like that.'

Just like the assistant, who'd faded away with no more than an envious glance in her direction, Diana recognised the imperative. He didn't need words to issue an order. He could do it with a look from those dark eyes.

'It's not good,' she warned him. 'Cinderella is, admittedly, a bit wet, but at least she's kind. And while Snow White is not exactly a female role model…'

'I don't have all day,' he warned.

'No, sir.' She took the globe and gave it a little shake to start the snowstorm. 'Okay, this is how it goes. Spoilt princess drops her precious golden ball in the well. The frog offers her a deal. If she takes him home with her, lets him eat from her plate, sleep on her pillow, kisses him goodnight…' She hesitated as, distracted by the sensuous curve of his lower lip, she lost the thread of the story.

'He's a talking frog?'

She shrugged. 'It's a fairy tale. If you want reality you're in the wrong place.'

He acknowledged the point with the slightest movement of his head. Then, 'Kisses him good-night,' he prompted.

'Mmm. If she promises all that,' she said, 'he'll fetch her golden ball from the bottom of the well.'

'A gentleman frog would have done it without strings attached.'

'A girl with any gumption would have got it herself.'

'You would have climbed down the well, Metcalfe?'

'I wouldn't have kissed the damn frog!'

'You disapprove?'

'There's no such thing as a free golden ball,' she said.

'No, indeed.' He did something with his eyes and, without warning, beneath the dark red uniform Diana suddenly felt very warm.

'Anyway,' she said quickly, running a finger under her collar to let in some cool air. 'She, um, agrees. Actually, she'd have promised him the moon—she loved that ball—and the ungentlemanly frog dives into the well, gets the ball and hands it over, at which point the princess shows her gratitude by legging it.'

'Legging it?'

'Has it away on her toes. Scarpers. Runs back to the palace without him.'

He laid one of those beautiful hands against his heart. 'I'm shocked.'

She'd been quite wrong about the irony. He 'got' it all right. He might not be laughing on the outside, but his eyes gleamed with amusement.

'I imagine the frog doesn't take that lying down?'

'As you said. The frog is no gentleman. He hops all the way to the palace, rats on the princess to the King, who tells her that a princess must always keep her word.'

'A princess shouldn't have to be told.'

'It might surprise you to know that holds good for common folk too.' Then, 'She isn't happy about it but she doesn't have much choice, so she lets him eat off her plate, but then she flounces off to bed without him.'

'She learns her lesson hard, this princess. Does the frog quit?'

'What do you think?'

'I think she's going to be sharing her pillow with the frog.'

'Right. It takes him hours to hop all the way up the stairs, find her room, but he gets there in the end and once more reminds her of her promise. Finally, accepting that she's beaten, the princess puts him on her pillow and even forces herself to kiss him goodnight.'

'I can relate to this frog, but can this story have a happy ending?'

'That rather depends on your point of view. When the princess wakes up next morning the frog has turned into a handsome prince.'

His brows rose a fraction.

'That might take a bit of explaining.'

Diana, whose view of the scene had been fixed in childhood by a picture book image of said handsome prince, fully clothed in princely trappings, standing beside the princess's bed as she woke, suddenly saw a very different reality and, quite stupidly, blushed.

'Yes, well,' she said quickly, 'it's that whole wicked-witch-cursing-the-handsome-prince thing. The princess had to have her arm twisted to breaking-point, but she did what was needed to break the spell. Da-da-de-da,' she sang the wedding march. 'And they all lived happily ever after.'

'You mean that now he's not a warty frog, but her equal, she marries him?'

'I did warn you. The girl is as shallow as an August puddle. It's why the prince married her that beats me.'

'Maybe the King didn't buy the "spell" story and produced a shotgun?' he offered.

'It's a nice theory, but the fact is that in fairy stories the girl always gets the prince. It's that love-at-first-sight, happy-ever-after thing.'

Zahir, hearing the scepticism in her voice, regarded her thoughtfully. 'You appear to be unconvinced,' he said.

'Do I?'

Metcalfe widened her eyes as if thinking about it. They weren't just green, he realised, but flecked with bronze.

'Maybe I am. You soon learn that it takes more than a handsome prince to provide a happy ending…'

He saw exactly the moment when it occurred to her that she might be heading for a foot-in-mouth moment. A reprise of the faint blush that had seared her cheek's a moment or two before. The nervous movement of her throat, as if trying to swallow down the words.

It was a refreshing change for someone to utterly forget who he was—say the first thing that came into her head without thinking it through.

'You'll get no argument from me,' he said, taking the globe from her, staring at her ringless fingers for a moment. No handsome prince, no happy ending for her. Although something warned him that it had been a lesson hard learned. 'In my country we do not pander to the sentimental Western view of marriage. Families arrange such things.'

'I can see how that would cut out an awful lot of emotional angst,' she said seriously. Then the dimple put in an appearance. 'Tough on frogs, though.'

'Indeed.' Turning swiftly to the display before the conversation became seriously out of hand, he said, 'So which of these heroines, in your opinion, is likely to provide the best role model for a modern princess? The "wet" one who stays at home and waits for a fairy godmother to wave a magic wand? The one who cleans up after a bunch of men who can't believe their luck? Or the princess who takes one look at the frog and takes to her heels?'

'Actually, I'm with you on this one. Forget the princess. That frog goes for what he wants and never gives up,' she said. 'He's a worthy role model for any child…'

He waited, certain that there was more.

'Any adult,' she added briskly.

'The frog it is. Shall we go and find that eager-to-please assistant? I have a feeling that she's panting to get busy with the gift-wrap and pink ribbons.'

Diana resisted the temptation to make a quick dash home while Sheikh Zahir delivered the birthday gift to Princess Ameerah.

All things being equal, there should have been time to make it there and back, and all that talk of happy-ever-after had left her in desperate need of a hug from Freddy before his grandma put him to bed.

But the last hour or so had been a bit of a roller-coaster ride—rather more down than up if she was brutally honest. Which was why, since 'equal' and London traffic had absolutely nothing in common, she didn't dare risk it, gladly accepting the footman's invitation to park in the mews behind the embassy and wait for the Sheikh in the comfort of the staff sitting room.

Fingers crossed, she'd managed to deliver the Sheikh to the embassy on an up; the schedule had allowed plenty of time for traffic hold-ups and, despite the delay for shopping and story-telling, her knowledge of the short cuts had meant that they'd only lost ten minutes.

But, despite his relaxed attitude, his inclination to dally over fairy tales, once he'd made a decision and headed for the cash desk, he'd appeared to forget she was there, saving all his charm for the assistant who'd gone to town with the ribbons, making it abundantly clear that he could have her gift-wrapped too. All he had to do was say the word.

No doubt it was an everyday occurrence for him since he had not, apparently, been tempted by the offer—a warning, not that she'd needed one, that it would be a mistake to take him, or his dangerous charm, seriously.

After they'd left the store he'd only spoken to her to confirm that he would be leaving the embassy at a quarter to seven. Exactly what she'd expect, in fact.

Stupid to take it personally.

This was a job, nothing more, and, left alone with a pot of tea, a sandwich and a choice of cake, she concentrated on her own life and used her cellphone to call home.

'Mummy!' Freddy's voice was full of excitement. 'I got a "good work" sticker for reading today!'

'Wow! I am *so* impressed.'

'I wanted to show you. Will you be home soon?'

Diana swallowed. It was so hard not to be there when he came out of school, to have him sharing these special moments with her parents instead of her. Not always being there to read him a story at bedtime.

But that was reality for all working mothers, not just the single ones. Sadie might have a nanny, but in every other way their situation was much the same— not enough hours in the day.

Even so, she knew she was luckier than most… Her parents might have been tight-lipped and angry when she'd got pregnant but they had supported her. And they loved Freddy.

'Will you?' he demanded.

'I've got to work this evening,' she said.

'O-o-h…' Then, 'Will you be home before I go to bed, Mummy?'

'I'll be there when you wake up,' she promised. 'Be good for Grandma and Grandpa, won't you?'

'Okay.'

'Big hug.'

'Oh, *Mum!*'

Make that dumb Mum, she thought as she drank the tea, bit into one of the sandwiches that had been brought for her—who knew when she'd get another chance?—going through every idiot thing she'd said and done since she'd collected Sheikh Zahir from the airport.

So much for 'politely invisible'.

What had she been *thinking?*

Huh! No prizes for getting that one right.

She hadn't been thinking at all. The only thing that had been working from the moment Sheikh Zahir had stepped through the arrivals hall door had been her mouth.

Okay, so he'd made it easy for her, had encouraged her even, but that didn't mean she had to dive in and make a total fool of herself.

Would she ever learn to think first? Speak… sparingly?

Not in this life, apparently…

At this rate she'd be bumping along on the bottom of the food-chain for ever instead of doing the job she was born for. Not driving a limousine, lovely though it was, but following in her dad's footsteps, driving a London Black Cab, where chat was all part of the job. Except that hers, as she'd so confidingly told Sheikh Zahir al Khatib, would not be boringly black, but pink.

She groaned.

That would be the same colour as her cheeks.

The discreet burble of her cellphone might have been a welcome distraction, except that the caller ID warned her that it was Sadie.

So much for talking herself out of trouble.

His Sheikhness had, presumably, called the office— or, more likely, got someone else to do it for him—to demand a driver with a proper peaked cap and a set of male chromosomes the minute she'd dropped him at the front door of the embassy. Someone who knew his place, understood the shopping requirements of the VIP and, more importantly, didn't talk the hind leg off a donkey given the slightest encouragement.

And he *had* encouraged her.

'Di?'

'Mmm… Yes. Sorry. I'm grabbing a sandwich…' She began to choke as she tried to swallow and talk at the same time. She'd let the boss down, had let herself down…

She'd promised to be good. Had promised that Sadie would hear about any problems from her. Who was she to criticize a princess who had run out on a frog?

'Okay, just listen. Apparently there's a broken water main in Grosvenor Place,' Sadie said, not waiting for her to gather herself, confess all. 'You'll need to cut down to Sloane Street to avoid it.'

What?

Sadie was calling to give her a traffic update? Not to demand an explanation for a priceless gift smashed beyond repair. Non-stop backchat. The shopping fiasco.

'Right,' she said, forcing down the egg and cress along with the lump in her throat. 'Thanks for letting me know.'

'I *was* expecting you to call me. I did ask you to keep in touch.'

'Every time I stop?' she asked, surprised. 'Does Jack have to check in every time he parks up?'

'You're not Jack.'

That was true. 'There's an up side to everything.'

'What's the down side?' Sadie said, instantly on to any suggestion of a problem.

'Nothing,' she said quickly. Then, 'Absolutely nothing.' And she allowed herself a small smile. The Sheikh hadn't split on her… 'We're running a bit late, that's all. Sheikh Zahir needed to shop.'

'Really?' Sadie instantly morphed from boss to woman at the "S" word. 'Where did you go? Aspreys? Garrard?'

'The Toy Warehouse.'

She didn't add that it had been her choice— probably just as well because there was a long pause before Sadie said, 'O-kaaay,' the last syllable stretched to breaking point. 'Well, I suppose that even a sheikh has ankle-biters to keep happy.'

'Not his,' she said quickly. Although, actually he hadn't confirmed or denied whether he had any children of his own. 'He wanted something for the Ambassador's daughter. It's her birthday.'

'As long as you kept him happy.'

'You'll have to ask him that.'

'I'm sure I'll hear soon enough if he's not.' Then, 'I called your father, by the way. He said he had it covered.'

On the point of reassuring Sadie that she'd already called home, she realised that she might not appreciate her priorities and left it at, 'Thank you.'

'You seem distracted, Zahir.' Hanif had drawn him to one side, away from the excitement of Ameerah as she showed her five-year-old brother and her little sister her new toy. Metcalfe had been right about the glass. It would not have done at all. 'Are there problems with the Nadira Creek project? Or the airline you're so keen to get off the ground?'

Zahir smiled. 'Business is never a problem, Han. Lucy's charities will not suffer.'

'Then it must be family. How is your father?'

'Pushing his pacemaker to the limits. He's in the Sudan this week, doing his best to broker peace...'

He lifted his hand in a helpless gesture. 'I cannot help but feel guilty. It should be me.'

'No, Zahir. Your talents lie elsewhere.'

'Maybe.'

'There's something else?'

Zahir looked across the room to where the five-year-old Jamal was watching Ameerah, entranced by the snowstorm. Then, turning back to Hanif, he said, 'He's impatient for a grandson to bear his name. Impatient with me for denying him that joy. I'm afraid I've been a disappointment to him in every aspect of my life.' He managed a smile. 'But not for much longer, it would seem. My mother has taken it upon herself to find me a bride.'

He'd anticipated wry amusement, but Hanif was not smiling. 'Marriage is a lifelong commitment, Zahir. Not something to be entered into lightly, even to gratify your father. And the timing could be better.'

'A point I made quite forcibly. My mother's response was that if I waited until I had time, it would never happen.' He shrugged. 'Along with a lot of other stuff about being wilful, selfish…'

'She's anxious to see you settled, Zahir. You may be wilful, but you're not selfish and she knows it. You surrendered more than two precious years to watch over me. You did that for the family.'

'I did it for you, Han. For you I would surrender my life.'

That finally brought a smile to his cousin's face. 'Surrendering your life is easy, Zahir. Take it from one who's been there. It's the living of it that takes effort.'

'No one could accuse me of neglecting that duty.' He worked hard, played hard, lived hard. 'But it's time to do something to show my feelings for him. Respect his wishes.'

'If it's written, *insh'Allah,* whether it is your mother's wish or your own, it will happen and I wish you happy of your bride.'

'You believe in fate?'

Hanif sounded so certain, but then he'd seen for himself how fate had tossed the lovely Lucy Forrester into his cousin's arms. Who could have foreseen that in his future?

Or that the deliciously curvy and delightfully offbeat Metcalfe would be at the wheel of his car today.

'Can I borrow Ameerah for a moment? My driver found her the snowstorm when my original gift was broken. I'd like her to know that it was appreciated.'

'Her?' Hanif's brow scarcely moved. But it moved.

Diana checked her watch. It was time to go and bring the car round to the front but, as she stood up, the sitting room door burst open and a lanky, olive-skinned, dark-haired girl launched herself through it.

'Thank you!' she exclaimed dramatically. 'Thank you so much for finding me the snowstorm. I absolutely love it!'

Diana, taken aback by such an over-the-top performance, looked up, seeking a responsible adult.

What she got was Sheikh Zahir, leaning on the door frame.

Oh. Right. This was his doing…

'I'm very glad you like it, Princess Ameerah. Are you having a lovely party?'

'Oh, we're not having a party today. I had school and Mummy has to go out tonight. We're going to take all my class out on Saturday. We're going on a canal boat trip to the zoo and having a picnic. I begged Zahir to come but he said that it's up to you.'

'Me?'

'You're his *driver!*'

'Oh, I see.'

Diana glanced up at the man leaning casually against the door frame. His expression was giving nothing away and yet she had the strongest impression that he was making a point. Reassuring her that she wouldn't be reduced to the minibus, perhaps?

'I promise,' she said, turning back to the child, 'that, whoever is driving Sheikh Zahir, he'll have absolutely no excuse not to be at your party.'

'You see!' Princess Ameerah, triumphant, swung round to face him. 'I told you it would be all right.'

'So you did.' He ruffled her curls. 'I'll see you on Saturday, Trouble.'

She ran off, but Zahir remained. '*Whoever* is driving?' he repeated.

'Jack Lumley will be back at work long before Saturday.'

'But do I want him when you're so much more entertaining?'

Entertaining!

'Please,' she begged, 'whatever you do, don't use that word if you speak to Sadie Redford. This is my big chance and I'm doing my best to be totally efficient, one hundred per cent VIP chauffeur material. As I'm sure you've noticed, I'm not a "natural" and if you suggest that I'm "entertaining" I'll be finished.'

'I won't say a word, Metcalfe, but it's not true, you know. Natural is exactly what you are.'

She made a valiant effort to keep the groan silent. She wasn't entirely successful.

'I know what I am. Not the first driver you'd think of if you were looking for someone to take the wheel of the newest limousine in Capitol's fleet.'

'You're doing just fine.' Then, before she was overcome with gratitude, 'Just promise that you

won't abandon me to the dull and efficient Jack
Lumley and I won't breathe a word about just how
"natural" you can get to Sadie Redford.'

She swallowed. 'You wouldn't…'

'Shall we go?'

Oh…sheikh…

'I'm just going to bring the car round,' she said and,
aiming for Miss Efficiency, checked her watch—
anything to avoid those dark, amused eyes that were
inviting her to be 'entertaining'. 'Five minutes?'

'Why don't I just come out the back way with
you?' he replied, standing back and inviting her to
lead the way. 'It'll save you having to drive round
the block, wasting precious natural resources.'

Was there the slightest stress on the 'natural', or
was she becoming paranoid?

Buttoning her lip, she fought down all and every
quip that sprang to her mind and neither of them
said another word until she pulled up at the entrance
to his hotel, where a top hatted commissionaire
opened the door.

'Seven forty-five, Metcalfe,' Sheikh Zahir said
as he stepped out.

'Yes, sir.'

Top Hat waved her into the parking bay reserved
for the privileged few. 'You can wait there.'

Her brain was saying, *Me? Really?*

Maybe it was shock, or maybe her lip was so

firmly buttoned up that the words couldn't escape. Instead, having managed a polite nod, she pulled over as if she'd expected nothing less.

It wasn't, after all, *personal*, she reminded herself. The honour was being bestowed on her passenger. On the car, even. On her Capitol uniform. It had absolutely nothing to do with her.

She called Sadie to reassure her that everything was still going according to plan and updated her on the traffic situation. Then she climbed out, walked around the car, duster in hand, checking for the slightest smear on the immaculate dark red paintwork, the gleaming chrome.

A couple of other chauffeurs nodded, passed the time of day, admiring her car, querying its handling, apparently accepting that, despite the missing chromosome, if someone had entrusted her with such a beast, she was one of them.

Maybe, she thought, she was the only one who was stopping that from being a fact. Living down to her image—single mother, relying on her parents for a roof over her head, help with childcare—rather than living up to her aspirations.

Maybe she'd become so used to hearing what she couldn't do, how limited her options were, that she'd begun to believe it.

Even the dream of owning her own taxi—where, as a teenager, she'd dreamed of owning a fleet of them, all pink, all with women drivers—had been reduced to little more than a family joke.

Next year you'll be driving your own taxi, Di...

Ho, ho, ho.

CHAPTER THREE

Summoned by the commissionaire, Diana was waiting at the kerb as Sheikh Zahir emerged from the hotel. This time he was not alone, but accompanied by a chisel-featured younger man blessed with the kind of cheekbones that could slice cheese.

Since he was the one carrying the laptop, he was, presumably, like her, a member of the 'bag-carrying' classes. Although, by the cut of his suit—and his hair—he outranked her by a considerable distance.

There was no mishap this time, probably because Top Hat was on hand to do the honours with the door and no one—not even a small boy—would have dared get in the way of his impressive figure.

The minute her passengers were settled she eased smoothly into the traffic, heading for the South Bank, managing, for once in her life, to remain 'politely anonymous'.

She had barely finished congratulating herself on this rare accomplishment when Sheikh Zahir said,

'Metcalfe, this is James Pierce. He's the man who makes everything work for me. You may, on occasion, be required to ferry him to appointments.'

'Sir,' she said, taking his tone from him. She was doing really well until, waiting for the lights to change, she made the mistake of glancing in the mirror and looking straight into his eyes. They did not match his voice. And his expression suggested that he wasn't fooled for a minute by her lapse into formality and her traitorous mouth let her down and smiled at him.

A mistake.

James Pierce, alerted by her response to the fact that she was not Jack Lumley, said, 'This is outrageous.' And he was looking at her when he said it.

Actually it couldn't just be the voice.

She didn't have one of those cut-glass BBC accents, but her mother had been a stickler for good diction and, apart from the occasional lapse, her speech could not, by any stretch of the imagination, be described as 'outrageous'.

It had to be the dimple, something she should have grown out of, along with the puppy fat. It was an embarrassment for anyone who expected to be taken seriously. Treated as a grown-up. Old enough to have a driving licence, let alone be behind the wheel of a limousine.

'When I made the booking with Capitol Cars I specifically requested…'

'Jack Lumley is sick,' Sheikh Zahir said, cutting him short.

'I'll call Sadie. She must have someone else available.'

Diana couldn't see James Pierce in the mirror, but from the moment he'd opened his mouth she did not like him and he wasn't doing one thing to change her mind.

His superior suit went with his attitude. She might be dumb enough to believe that they were on the same side, but he wasn't buying it. But then a man 'who makes everything work' for a billionaire sheikh probably wasn't.

'Why would we need someone else?' Sheikh Zahir intervened. 'Metcalfe is a—'

Please, please not 'natural' she begged silently, as the lights began to change and she had no choice but to check the mirror. He was still looking at her. Only his eyes changed, the rest of his face remained grave; the smile, she realised, was for her alone.

'—thoroughly competent driver.'

He knew, she thought. He knew exactly what she was thinking and he was teasing her, making her complicit in an intimate conspiracy against the stuffed shirt.

Without warning a warmth, starting somewhere around her abdomen, seeped through every cell of her body until she felt her cheeks begin to flush.

Fortunately, Sheikh Zahir had turned away.

'Don't tell me you're one of those dinosaurs who feel emasculated when driven by a woman, James,' he said, teasing him a little too.

'No…' His reply was unconvincing. 'No, of course not.'

'I'm very glad to hear that. As a lawyer, even if your field is corporate law, I know you wouldn't want to give Metcalfe an excuse to sue the pants off you for sexual discrimination.'

'I just thought—'

'I know what you thought, James, but as you are well aware, it's not a problem.'

He didn't wait for an answer, but immediately turned his attention to business, launching into some complex legal question regarding a lease.

It was an example she'd be wise to follow, she decided. Flirting through the rear-view mirror with a passenger was definitely not the action of a 'thoroughly, competent driver'. Quite the contrary.

Someone who was entertaining now…

Oh, stop it!

At the entrance to the Riverside Gallery, she climbed out and opened the door, keeping her eyes front and centre.

James Pierce stepped out of the car and walked past her without a word or a look. The word 'miffed' crossed her mind—one of her mother's favourite words to describe someone who'd had their nose put out of joint.

Sheikh Zahir paused and, realising that she was grinning, she swiftly straightened her face.

'What will you do until you pick us up, Metcalfe?'

'I've got a book,' she said quickly. Her message— *competent* chauffeurs were used to waiting around. They were ready for it.

Not actually true—the kind of jobs she was usually assigned didn't leave a lot of spare time to catch up on her reading—but he was just being polite and she'd make sure she had one with her tomorrow. Always assuming there was a tomorrow.

Maybe it was time to start brushing up on her Blue Book—the taxi drivers' bible that listed the shortest runs from a given point to any destination, the 'Knowledge' which had to be passed before a "cabbie" could get a licence.

Still he lingered. 'There's no reason why you shouldn't come into the gallery. Have something to eat. You could look at the pictures if the presentation bores you.'

Jolted out of her firm resolve not to make eye contact, she looked up. Swallowed. His smile had progressed to his mouth, tugging at one corner, lifting it a fraction, and something in the region below her ribcage flickered in response, taking her by surprise.

She covered the little gasp with a breathy, 'Th-thank you.' Then, firmly resisting the temptation to be led astray for the second time that day—he had chisel-cheeks to carry his bags, after all—she said, 'I really should…'

'Stay with the car?' he finished for her, saving her from wavering.

'It's advisable.' She gave an apologetic little shrug, then nodded in the direction of the gallery, cleared her throat and said, 'Mr Pierce is waiting for you, sir.'

'Zahir.'

'Sir?'

'Everyone who works for me calls me Zahir. It's the modern way, I'm told. It's not a mile away from "sir", so maybe, if you tried very hard, you might manage it.'

'Yes, sir.'

The smile fading, he nodded, 'Enjoy your book, Metcalfe.'

She watched him walk away. Still no flowing robes, just the standard male uniform of a dark suit, silk tie, although on Sheikh Zahir, she had to admit, it looked anything but standard.

Zahir.

She'd had the name in her head ever since Sadie had hauled her out of the minibus. Alone, she tried it on her tongue, her lips.

'Zahir…'

Exotic.

Different.

Dangerous…

She shivered a little as the breeze came off the river, sweeping over the acres of concrete paving.

Snatches of jazz reached her from a party on boat cruising down the river and, despite the chill, she tugged off her gloves and hat and tossed them on to her seat. Then, having locked the car, she walked across to the railing that ran alongside the river, leaning her elbows on it, looking across at the familiar skyline, dominated by the dome of St Paul's.

Focus, Diana, she told herself. *Keep on your toes. This is not the time for playing dangerous games. No first name nonsense with the handsome prince. Fairy tales are for children.*

This could be an opportunity to take a step up, earn enough to make your own dream into reality. Don't mess it up just because the prince has a pair of dark eyes that look at you as if…

Forget *if!*

She'd done dark and dangerous and wasn't making the same mistake again.

Freddy, her little boy, was her entire world. His future was in her hands, her duty was to him before anyone.

And, if that didn't concentrate her mind, then all

she'd have to do was remember the way the bank manager had looked at her when she'd done what their seductive advertisements on the television had encouraged her to do and had applied for a loan to buy a cab, start her own business. His four point response:

1 Single mother.
2 No bricks and mortar, not even ones mort-gaged to the hilt as collateral.
3 No assets of any kind.
4 No thanks.

He might as well have patted her on the head and told her to run along. At the time she'd been so angry. Had promised herself she'd be back…

Two years later and she was still no closer to impressing him. And if she was idiot enough to lose her head over a sexy smile twice, then she'd only prove that he'd been right.

Zahir finished his brief presentation to the gathering of tour operators and travel journalists and was immediately buttonholed by the CEO of a top-of-the-range tour company, who was examining the display of photographs and the architect's model of the Nadira Resort.

'This is an interesting concept, Zahir. Different. Exactly the sort of thing our more discerning travellers are looking for. I imagine it's going to be expensive?'

'Reassuringly so,' he said, knowing it was what the man wanted to hear. 'Why don't you talk to James? He's organising a site visit and we'd love to show you what we're offering.'

Zahir moved on, shaking hands, answering questions, issuing personal invitations to the hand-picked group of travel journalists and tour operators as he went.

Then the woman he was talking to moved to one side to let a waitress pass and he found himself looking straight out of one of the gallery's tall, narrow windows. The car was still there, but Metcalfe was nowhere to be seen.

No doubt she was curled up on the back seat with her book. Maybe he could catch her out, watch as, blushing with confusion, she scrambled to straighten that ridiculous hat.

He'd enjoy that.

But she wouldn't.

Metcalfe.

He'd offered his name, hoping for hers in return. She'd known it too and, wisely, had taken a step back from his implicit invitation to become something more than his driver. Well aware that, whatever 'more' he was offering, it wasn't going to be something she would be interested in. And how could he tell her that she was wrong when he didn't know himself what that was?

Or maybe he was fooling himself. They both knew. Had both responded to that instant, unfathomable chemistry…

Maybe James was right after all. Lumley might be dull but he wasn't distracting. He wouldn't have given a moment's thought about how he'd spend his time in the gaps between engagements. He certainly wouldn't have asked him to come into the gallery, been eager to show him what he was doing. Talk about his plans…

'Is your neutral energy target realistic, Sheikh Zahir?' the woman prompted. 'Really?'

'We're fortunate that solar energy is a year-round resource in Ramal Hamrah, Laura,' he said, forcing himself to concentrate on the job in hand. He'd taken the time and trouble to memorize the names and faces of the people he was to meet. 'I do hope you'll come and see for yourself.'

'Well, that's the other problem, isn't it? How can you justify expanding your tourist industry at a time when air travel is being cited as a major cause of carbon emission?'

'By developing a new kind of airline?' he offered with a smile. Then, remembering Metcalfe's wry comment when he'd done the same thing in the toy store, regretted it. With a glance, he summoned James to his side. 'James, Laura Sommerville is the Science Correspondent for *The Courier*...'

'Laura...' James smoothly gathered her up, enabling Zahir to excuse himself.

He tried not to look at his watch.

He was tiring of this kind of public relations exercise. His dreams were bigger these days. He was happier in the background, planning for the future. He had to find someone else to be the public face of this part of the business so that he could take a step back. Someone capable of fuelling the buzz of interest that would give his pet project wings.

Or maybe his desire to be somewhere else had less to do with ennui, more to do with wanting to be with someone else, he thought, doing his best not to snatch another glance out of the window. And failing.

Maybe it had everything to do with his unexpected, his unusual, his very lovely young chauffeur.

Distracted by a movement near the river, he saw that, far from being curled up with a book, Metcalfe was standing at the riverside railing, watching the lights come on across the river as dusk gathered. Hatless, her hair had been whipped loose by the breeze and, arms raised, she was attempting to twist it back into a knot...

A waitress paused in front of him with a tray, cutting off his view, and he moved to one side so that he did not lose sight of her as her jacket lifted, her shirt parted company with her waistband and she bared an inch of skin.

'Canapé, sir?'

'Sorry?'

Then, registering what the waitress had said, he looked at her. Looked at the tray.

'Thank you,' he said and, having taken the tray, he headed for the door.

'Some watchdog you are, Metcalfe. Anyone could have driven off with your precious car.'

Diana, who, despite all her best efforts, had been thinking about this extraordinarily beautiful man who'd invaded her thoughts, her life, jumped at the unexpected sound of his voice.

'They could try,' she said. 'Of course, if they got past the locks and the alarm, there is still the global positioning gizmo.'

'Those gizmos will get you every time,' he said, joining her at the rail. Then, 'So why didn't you come into the gallery?'

'Mr Pierce would not have approved,' she said, keeping her eyes fixed firmly on the north bank of the Thames. 'Besides, this view is more interesting than a load of old paintings.'

'"…all that mighty heart…"' he prompted.

'Wordsworth had it nailed, didn't he?' Unable to

help herself, she glanced at him. 'How many Englishmen could quote an Arabic poet, I wonder?' Then, before he could embarrass them both by answering, 'Did the party end prematurely?'

'No, it's in full swing.'

'Oh.' He'd come out to see her. She looked at the tray. He'd brought her food? 'Does Mr Pierce know you've escaped?'

'Escaped?'

'You *are* the star attraction?'

'On the contrary, the Nadira Resort is the star of the show. Besides, I distracted James with a serious young journalist who doubts my probity.'

'Why?'

He offered her the tray. 'I thought you might be hungry.'

She stared at it for a moment, then, with a little shake of her head, said, 'No, why does she doubt your probity? Whatever that is.'

'Maybe integrity is a better word.' Then, 'You know journalists. Natural cynics.'

'That's one word for it.' Then, 'Why would she believe James Pierce and not you?'

'She won't. His job is to persuade her to come to Nadira and see the resort for herself.'

A smile from him would have been enough, she thought. One of his smiles could get him anything he wanted…

'Cynicism pays, then. Nice work…' she said, pushing the thought away. Not *anything*. Not her snow globe. Not *her.* 'If you'd said you were handing out free holidays, even I might have been…'

Tempted.

She left the word unspoken, but they both knew what she had been going to say. Embarrassed, she focused on the selection of canapés laid out on the tray—all the temptation she was prepared to indulge in.

'These look good enough to eat,' she said.

'Help yourself.'

The words sounded…loaded. An invitation to do more than take one of the exquisite little savouries. She forced herself to take the words literally. She wasn't hungry, but filling her mouth with food would at least prevent her from saying anything she'd regret.

Saying anything.

The small pastry she took exploded in her mouth, leaving a soft, warm centre of cheese. She wasn't totally acting when she groaned with pleasure.

'Have you tried one of those?'

'Should I?' Zahir asked seriously.

'Yes… No! Definitely not. You should leave them all for me and go back to your party.'

He took one, tried it for himself. 'I see what you mean,' he said, sucking a dribble of cheese from the pad of his thumb, leaving a crumb clinging to his lower lip, drawing quite unnecessary attention to it.

It was all she could do to stop herself from reaching up and wiping it away with her fingers.

Nothing in the world could prevent her from imagining doing it.

'Why don't we take this over to that bench?' he suggested. 'If we're going to do this justice we need to sit down.' Then, 'I should have brought us something to drink.'

'Us? Excuse me, but won't you be missed?'

'You want all this for yourself, is that it?' The words were serious, his expression anything but, and she laughed. It was so easy to laugh when he looked at her like that.

'You've got me bang to rights, guv,' she said.

'Help yourself. I've still got dinner to get through.'

He didn't sound particularly excited by the prospect of dining at one of London's most exclusive restaurants.

'I wouldn't have thought that was exactly a strain.'

'Fine food ruined by high finance. A recipe for indigestion.'

'That's what you get for mixing business with pleasure.'

'How wise you are, Metcalfe. What a pity the money men aren't as sensible.'

'I guess they take the view that time is money, so

doing two things at once is earning them twice as much.'

'Especially if they're not paying for dinner.'

'Good point.'

He set the tray down, waited for her to sit and, having apparently debated with himself for a moment, sat on the far side of it so that it was between them. She couldn't decide if she was relieved or disappointed…

'I love this view, don't you?' Zahir said, saving her from having to admit to disappointment. 'So much history packed into every square metre.'

'You've spent a lot of time in London?'

'Too much,' he admitted cheerfully as he leaned back and stretched out his long legs. 'I was at school just up the river.'

'Really? Me, too.' Then, catching on to exactly which school 'up the river' he was talking about, she said, 'Obviously, in my case, it wasn't Eton, but the local comprehensive. In Putney.'

'Is that where you live now?'

'Mmm.' She stuffed in another taste sensation—this time something involving smoked salmon and sour cream—and shrugged. 'Twenty-three years old and still living at home,' she said, brushing the crumbs from her fingers. 'How sad can you get?'

'Sad?'

'Pathetic. Dull.'

'On the contrary. It is the way it should be. Women in my country live under the protection of their families until they're married.'

Not if they had a five-year-old son and no husband they didn't, Diana thought as, for a moment, they just looked at one another, confronting the gulf between them.

Zahir knew he should move. Stop this—whatever *this* was. While he was sitting here flirting with his chauffeur, wanting to do much more, his mother, his sisters, were sifting through the Ramal Hamrah equivalent of the 'girls in pearls' to choose his perfect bride...

Even as he urged himself to move, a gust of wind tugged at Metcalfe's hair, whipping a strand across her face and, acting purely on instinct, he reached out to capture it.

Silk, he thought, as it tangled in his fingers, brushed against his wrist. Chestnut-coloured silk, a perfect counter to the bronze-flecked green of eyes that widened, darkened as he looked down at her, and the temptation to wrap it round his fist and draw her closer almost overwhelmed him.

Almost. He was not so lost...

Slowly, taking care not to touch her cheek, he gathered it, then was left with no alternative but to tuck it behind her ear. Her ear, the smooth, fine skin of her neck, undid all his best intentions. The warmth drew him in, held him captive, and he spread his hand to cradle her head.

Until the last second she watched him, eyes wide as a fawn, but the second before his lips met hers she slammed them shut, caught her breath and, for the longest moment in his life, she was rigid, unmoving. Then she melted and kissed him back.

It was the crash of the tray that brought them both to their senses.

Metcalfe jerked away with a little gasp, looking at him for a moment, eyes wide, mouth full and dark, cheeks flushed, everything she was feeling on display. As if she knew, she looked away, glancing down at the tray.

'Pigeon heaven,' she said, breaking the silence, as the birds began to snatch at the scattered food.

He wanted to say something, but what? He couldn't even say her name. Metcalfe wouldn't do…

'I have to get back to the gallery,' he said, getting to his feet.

She nodded. 'I'll bring back the tray.' Then, when he still didn't make a move, she looked up at him and said, 'Diana. My name is Diana Metcalfe.'

'Like the princess?'

'I'm afraid so. My mother was a fan.'

'Diana was also a goddess.'

'I know. It's really rather more of a name than one

very ordinary girl could ever hope to live up to.' She swallowed. 'Most people just call me Di.'

'There's no such thing as an ordinary girl, Diana. Each person is unique, individual.' Then, with a touch of anger, 'The world is full of people ready to keep you in what they perceive to be your place. Don't give them a head start by doing it to yourself.'

Diana stared at him for a moment, but he hadn't waited for her answer. With something that was more than a nod, less than a bow, he turned and walked quickly away.

Was he angry with her?

He needn't bother. Give her a moment to gather her wits, forget a touch that had stirred her to the core, waking feelings, desires she had thought stone dead, and she'd be angry enough for both of them.

As for that stuff about her 'place'. Easy to say, when your own place in the world was so far above ordinary that you probably needed an oxygen mask.

What did he know about her life?

Single mother at eighteen. And then, just as she might have turned her life around, her father had been disabled by a stroke, leaving her and her mother having to work full-time, run as fast as they could just to keep in the same place. All dreams on hold for the duration.

Tomorrow she'd bring sandwiches and a flask of

tea as well as her standard bottle of water—the full 'chauffeur' kit—she promised herself, picking up the tray and tossing the remainder of the canapés to the pigeons.

Always assuming Zahir hadn't given James Pierce the nod to do what he'd wanted from the moment he'd set eyes on her and organise another driver. For both their sakes.

'Great start, Diana,' she said to herself. 'Professional, eh? Well, that's a joke.' Cheek and chat were one thing, but kissing the client? 'Failed on every count.'

Even if he didn't pull the plug, she knew she should phone Sadie right now and do it for him. But she didn't. Instead she walked across to the gallery on legs that felt as if they were walking on feathers. Handed the tray over to a waitress, taking care to look neither to left nor right as she headed for the ladies' to wash her hands.

But when, a few minutes later, she emerged, the first person she saw, through a gap in the crowd, was Zahir. She could have just put her head down and scurried out, but there was not a chance in the world that he would notice her, flirt with her. His attention was totally engaged by a tall, elegant blonde, her long cream-coloured hair twisted up in a simple stylish twist. Not some foolish girl, but a beautiful woman. Not wearing a hideous uniform, but an exquisitely embroidered *shalwar kameez*, the kind that cost telephone numbers.

As Diana stood there, temporarily mesmerised, the woman smiled and touched his arm in a gesture of casual intimacy. There was a relaxed easiness between them and she didn't doubt that they knew each other well.

It was as if she'd been slapped on the side of the head, given a reality check.

Sheikh Zahir was a man who would draw beautiful women to him like a magnet. Beautiful women in beautiful clothes, stunningly high-heeled designer shoes.

He'd kissed her because she was there. Because he could. It was what men did. They took what was on offer without a thought, nothing engaged but their hormones.

For heaven's sake, she only had to *look* at him to see how it was. Remember the drooling reaction of the assistant in the toy store.

As for her, well, she was undoubtedly giving out all the same signals and he'd responded to them the same way he breathed. Instinctively.

It had happened to her once before and she knew it didn't mean a thing. Not a thing, she thought, turning away and finding herself face to face with James Pierce.

He glanced across at his boss, then back at her,

and, as if he'd known exactly what she was thinking, he gave her a pitying smile and said, 'She's lovely, isn't she?'

'Lovely,' she managed. Then, unable to help herself, 'Who is she?'

'His partner.' Then, while her brain was processing that piece of information, 'You'd better get back to the car. Sheikh Zahir will be leaving in five minutes.'

She needed no encouragement to leave, escaping into the fresh air where she dragged in steadying breaths as she replaced her hat, her gloves, donning them as if they were armour.

She'd expected the blonde to be with him, but when, a few moments later, Zahir emerged, he was alone but for James Pierce.

'I'll leave you to mop up the stragglers, James. I want every one of these people to visit Nadira, experience it firsthand.'

'I've got all but a couple of broadsheet journalists who want to be coaxed but the princess will have them eating out of her hands before they know it.'

The blonde was a princess?

Why was she surprised?

'No doubt. In my absence, will you see Lucy safely to her car?'

'It will be my pleasure.' Then, 'I'll be on call should Lord…' James Pierce glanced at her, leaving the name unsaid, making it crystal clear that he doubted her discretion.

'Thank you, James. I think I can handle any query Lord Radcliffe is likely to raise,' Zahir replied, demonstrating that he had no such qualms.

Well, he'd kissed her. She was, presumably, at now his beck and call.

'Berkeley Square, Diana?' he prompted, as he stepped into the car.

'Sir,' she said.

'Come back and collect me as soon as you've dropped off Sheikh Zahir, Metcalfe,' James Pierce said sharply.

Sheikh Zahir held out a hand, stopping her from closing the door. 'Take a taxi, James.'

'It's no trouble,' Diana said quickly, not wanting to give the stuffed shirt any reason to complain to Sadie, determined to show him that nothing had changed. 'I'll only be sitting around, waiting.' She summoned a smile, the polite variety, for James Pierce. 'I'll be as quick as I can, Mr Pierce.'

She climbed behind the wheel, started the car and, using her wing mirrors, taxi-driver style, she made her way through London managing to avoid any possibility of eye-contact with her passenger.

And, since she was working strictly to the 'don't speak until spoken to' rule, it was a silent journey since Sheikh Zahir said nothing.

He was probably angry because she'd had the temerity to intervene over his suggestion that James Pierce take a taxi. He probably wasn't used to anyone arguing with him, although anyone with any sense could see that it had to be more sensible to be doing something, even transporting chisel-cheeks, than just hanging around waiting for him to talk his way through dinner. Or maybe, once kissed, she had joined his personal harem and was now his alone.

'Tosh, Diana,' she muttered under her breath. 'One kiss and you're losing it…'

And yet he didn't move to get out of the car by himself when she'd eased around Berkeley Square and pulled up in front of the restaurant.

Was that his way of making the point that it had changed nothing? Or everything?

Apparently neither. He was so far lost in his thoughts as she opened the door that it was obvious he hadn't even noticed that they'd stopped.

'What time would you like me to pick you up, sir?' she asked, taking no chances.

Zahir had spent the journey from the Riverside Gallery gathering his thoughts for the coming meeting. Trying to block out the image, the taste, the scent of the woman sitting in front of him. All it took was a word, a solemn enquiry, to undo all that effort.

'If you're not sure, maybe you could call me?' She took a card from her jacket pocket and offered it to him. 'When you've got to the coffee stage of the evening?'

It was a standard Capitol card. 'Call you?'

'That's the car phone number printed on the front,' she said. 'I've printed my cellphone number on the back.'

He took the card, still warm from her body, and, to disguise the sudden shake of his fingers, he turned it over and looked at the neatly printed numbers. It was, had always been, his intention to walk back to his hotel. He knew he'd need a little time to clear his head, no matter what the outcome of his meeting. On the point of telling her that she could go home, that she could have gone now if she hadn't insisted on picking up James, he stopped himself. Sending her home early might make him feel good, but he'd be doing her no favours. On the contrary, he'd be robbing her of three hours' work at the highest evening rate.

'Eleven-thirty should do it,' he said. 'If there's a change of plan, I'll give you a call.'

'Yes, sir.'

The 'sir' jabbed at him. But it wasn't just the 'sir'. For the first time since she'd handed him the broken toy outside the airport, she wasn't quite looking at him. She had her gaze firmly fixed on something just over his right shoulder and it occurred to him that Diana, with considerable grace, was telling him that she understood that his kiss had meant nothing. Giving him—giving them both—the chance to step back. Go back to the beginning. To the moment before an excited child had altered everything.

He could do no less. Acknowledging her tact with the slightest of bows, he said, 'Thank you, Metcalfe.'

CHAPTER FOUR

FOR the briefest moment Diana met his gaze. For the briefest moment he saw something in her eyes that made him forget the powerful men who were waiting for him, forget his precious airline. All he felt was a rush of longing, an overwhelming need to stop Diana from driving away, climb back into the car beside her and take her somewhere quiet, intimate, where their separate worlds, his and hers, did not exist.

But to what purpose?

For her smile? To watch it appear, despite every attempt she made to control it?

To listen to her, enjoy conversation that had no ulterior purpose. No agenda.

She might laugh, blush, even share a kiss, but with that swift return to 'sir' she had recognised the gulf between them even if he, in a moment of madness, had chosen to ignore it. She knew—they both knew—that in the end all they could ever share was a brief intimacy that had no future. Kind enough to take a step back, pretend that it had never happened, when a more calculating woman would have seen a world of possibilities.

Selling a kiss-and-tell sheikh-and-the-chauffeur story to one of the tabloids would have paid for her dream twice over. That sparkly pink taxi for weekdays and something really fancy for Sunday. And he knew all about dreams…

If she could do that for him, why was he finding it such a problem to do it for himself?

It wasn't as if he was in the habit of losing his head, or his heart, over a sweet smile.

He might have a streak of recklessness when it came to business, even now be prepared to risk everything he'd achieved. But he'd been far more circumspect in his personal life, taking care to keep relationships on a superficial level, with women who played by the same rules he did—have fun, move on—who understood that his future was written, that there was no possibility of anything deeper, anything permanent between them. Who would not get hurt by a light-hearted flirtation.

Diana Metcalfe was not one of those women.

And he did not feel light-hearted.

Yet, even when he recognised the need for duty before pleasure, he still wanted to hear his name on her lips, wanted to carry her smile with him.

Couldn't rid himself of the scent of her skin, the sweet taste of her that lingered on his lips, a smile than went deeper the more he looked, a smile that faded to a touch of sadness.

He'd need all his wits about him this evening if he was going to pull off the biggest deal of his career to date and all he could think about was what had made the light go out of her eyes. *Who* had made the light go out of her eyes...

And, on an impulse, he lifted the card he was still holding, caught a trace of her scent. Nothing that came from a bottle, but something warm and womanly that was wholly Diana Metcalfe.

He stuffed it into his pocket, out of sight, dragged both hands through his hair, repeating his earlier attempt to erase the tormenting thoughts. He should call James right now and tell him to contact the hire company and ask them to provide another driver for tomorrow. Maybe, if she was out of sight, he could put her out of his mind.

But even that escape was denied him.

His first mistake, and it had been entirely his, was not to have kissed her, not even to have allowed himself to be distracted by her; he'd have to have been made of wood not to have been distracted by her. His first mistake had been to talk to her. Really talk to her.

He'd talked to Jack Lumley, for heaven's sake,

but he'd known no more about the man after a week in his company than he had on day one.

Diana didn't do that kind of polite, empty conversation.

He'd said she was a 'natural', but she was more than that. Her kind of natural didn't require quotation marks. Diana Metcalfe was utterly unaffected in her manner. Spoke first, thought second. There was no fawning to please. None of the schooled politeness that the Jack Lumleys of this world had down to a fine art.

He wouldn't, couldn't, ruin her big chance, send her back to the 'school run' when she'd done nothing wrong.

He was the one breaking all the rules and he was the one who'd have to suffer.

Maybe an evening brokering the kind of financial package required to launch an airline would have much the same effect as a cold shower, he thought as he watched the tail lights of the car disappear.

Or maybe he just needed to get a grip.

'Excellency.' The *maître d'* greeted him warmly as he led the way to a private dining room, booked for this very discreet dinner. 'It's good to see you again.'

'And you, Georges.'

But as he followed him up the wide staircase he deliberately distanced himself from this international, cosmopolitan world. Reminded himself with every step of his own culture, his own future. Demonstrated it by enquiring after the man's family, his wife, not as he'd learned to do in the west, but in the Arab manner, where to mention a man's wife, his daughters, would be an insult.

'How are your sons?' he asked, just as his father, his grandfather would have done.

Diana drove back to the yard, filled in her log, wrapped the shattered remains of the snow globe in a load of newspaper before disposing of it. Vacuum cleaned the inside of the car.

Even managed a bite of the sandwich she'd picked up at the local eight-'til-late.

But keeping her hands busy did nothing to occupy her brain. That was away with the fairies and would keep reliving that moment when he'd kissed her and, for just a moment, she'd felt like a princess.

Zahir had wanted to send Diana away, had planned to call at eleven and tell her to go home, but somehow the moment had passed and when, leaving the restaurant, he saw her waiting for him, he knew that his subconscious had sabotaged his good intentions. And could not be anything but glad.

It wasn't solitude he needed at this moment, but the company of someone with whom he could share his excitement. Someone who had a smile that reached deep inside him and heated him to the heart.

'You've had a long day, Metcalfe. Can you spare another five minutes?'

'Yes… Yes, of course. Where do you want to go?'

'Nowhere. Will you walk around the square with me?'

Maybe he'd got the formula right this time, or maybe she caught something of the excitement he'd had to suppress in the presence of the financiers, but which was now fizzing off him. Whatever it was, she clicked the key fob to secure the car and fell in beside him.

'There are no stars,' he said, looking up. 'The light pollution in London robs you of the sky. If we were in the desert the night would be black, the stars close enough to touch.'

'It sounds awesome.' Then, as he glanced at her, 'I meant…'

'I know what you meant,' he said. She wasn't using teenage slang, but using the word as it was meant to be used. 'And you're right. It's empty. Cold. Clean. Silent but for the wind. It fills a man with awe. Reminds him how small he is. How insignificant.'

'Did your meeting not go well?' she asked anxiously.

'Better than I could ever have imagined.' A rare take-it-or-leave-it arrogance had carried him through dinner tonight. He'd cut through the waffle and, refusing to play the games of bluff and counter-bluff, had gone straight to the bottom line, had told them what he wanted, what he was prepared to offer. Maybe his passion had convinced them. 'Beyond the four of us at dinner tonight, you are the first to know what the world will hear two days from now. That Ramal Hamrah is about to have its own airline.'

'Oh.' Then, 'That is big.'

'Every deal is big, only the numbers change.' Then, looking down at her, 'When you buy your pink taxi it will be huge.'

'It'll be a miracle,' she said with feeling, 'but, if it ever happens, I promise you that I'll look up at the stars and remind myself not to get too big for my boots.'

He took her arm as they crossed the road and, when they reached the safety of the footpath, he tucked it safely beneath his before once more looking up at the reddish haze of the sky and said, 'Not in London, Metcalfe.' For a moment she'd frozen, but maybe his use of her surname reassured her and, as she relaxed, he moved on. 'I suppose you could go to the Planetarium.'

'Not necessary. In London you don't look up to see the stars. You look down.' He frowned and she laughed. 'Didn't you know that the streets of London aren't paved with gold, they're paved with stars.'

'They are?'

He looked down and then sideways, at her. 'Obviously I'm missing something.'

'We're in Berkeley Square?' she prompted.

'And?'

'You've never heard the song?' She shook her head. 'Why would you? It's ancient.'

Berkeley Square… Something snagged in his memory, a scratchy old record his grandfather used to play. 'I thought it was about a nightingale.'

'You do know it!

'I remember the tune.' He hummed a snatch of it and she smiled.

'Almost,' she said, laughing. 'But it's not just the nightingale. There's a line in there about stars too.' She lifted her shoulders in an awkward little shrug. 'My dad used to sing it to my mum,' she said, as if she felt she had to explain how she knew. 'They used to dance around the kitchen…'

'Really?' He found the idea enchanting. 'Like this?' And as he turned his arm went naturally to her waist. 'Well, what are you waiting for? Sing…' he commanded.

Diana could not believe this was happening. There were still people about—Zahir's kind of people, men in dinner jackets, women in evening clothes—heading towards the fashionable nightclubs in the area to celebrate some special occasion. Laughing, joking, posing as someone took photographs with a camera phone.

Maybe if she'd been dressed in a glamorous gown she wouldn't have felt so foolish. But in her uniform…

'Don't!' she begged, but Zahir caught her hand and, humming, began to spin her along the footpath. 'Zahir…' Then, 'For heaven's sake, that's not even the right tune!'

'No? How does it go?'

Maybe his excitement, his joy, were infectious, but somehow, before she knew it, she was singing it to him, filling gaps in the words with 'da-da-de-dum's and he was humming and they were dancing around Berkeley Square to a song that was old when her parents had first danced to it. A song in which the magic of falling in love made the impossible happen. Made London a place where angels dined, where nightingales sang and where the streets were paved with stars.

Dancing as if they were alone in the universe and the streets truly were paved with stars.

It was only when she came to the end of the song that she realised they had stopped dancing, that they were standing by the car. That Zahir was simply holding her.

That what she wanted more than anything in the world was for him to kiss her again.

And as if reading her thoughts, he raised her hand to his lips, before tilting his head as if listening to something very faint.

'Can you hear it?' he murmured. 'The nightingale.'

It was a question that asked more than whether she could, impossibly, hear a shy woodland bird singing in a London square.

It took every atom of common sense to ignore the soft touch of his breath against her cheek, his fingers still wrapped about hers, his hand warm against her waist. To ignore the magic of the nightingale's sweet song filling her heart.

It took Freddy's voice saying, 'Will you be home before I go to bed, Mummy?' The memory of her promise, 'I'll be there when you wake up.'

'No, sir,' she managed, her voice not quite her own. 'I think you'll find that's a sparrow.'

And with that she shattered the fragile beauty of the moment and the danger passed. He took a step back and said, with the gravest of smiles, 'I forgot, Metcalfe. You don't believe in fairy stories.'

For a moment she wanted to deny it. Instead, she said, 'Neither, sir, do you.'

'No.' He repeated the touch of his lips to her finger and, without a word, turned and began to walk away.

What?

'Sir!' He did not seem to hear her. 'Where are you going?' Then, in desperation, 'Zahir!'

Without stopping, without turning, he said, 'Go home, Metcalfe. I'll walk back to the hotel.'

'But…'

He stopped. Looked up to a sky fogged with neon. *But? But what? What was she thinking?*

As if in answer to her unspoken question, he turned and, as their eyes met, she knew 'what'.

She'd always known.

She'd been here before and the raw power of the heat-charged look that passed between them scared her witless.

She'd had the sense to take a step back and then, as if seized by a determination to destroy herself all over again, she'd undone it all with that 'but'.

And she had no excuse. She wasn't an eighteen-year-old with her head in the clouds and her brains in cold storage. At eighteen there was some excuse. At twenty-three, with her reputation rebuilt, responsibilities...

She was fooling herself.

This was desire at its most primitive. The atavistic urge that powered all of creation. Age, experience, counted for nothing. There was no immunity...

'But?' Zahir finally prompted, his voice as soft as thistledown.

Without thought she'd reached out to him. Her hand was still extended, as if imploring him to come back. Finish what he'd started.

Slowly, deliberately, she closed her hand, but somehow it stayed there and he took a step towards her.

Maybe the movement broke the spell. Maybe age did help, because she swung her arm wildly towards the far corner of the square. 'You're going the wrong way,' she said. 'You need Charles Street. Then, um, Queen Street. Then Curzon Street.'

'That's out of the taxi drivers' handbook, is it?'

'Yes. No…' Her eyes were still locked on to his. She could scarcely breathe. 'Queen Street is one-way. I'd…a taxi…would have to cut along Erfield Street.'

Zahir gently took her arm, opened the driver's door of the car and said, 'I'll see you in the morning, Diana. Ten o'clock.'

Zahir stood back as she climbed into the limo, fumbled to get the key in the ignition and, after what seemed like an age, drove away. Only then did he let loose the breath he seemed to have been holding for ever.

He'd only met the woman a few hours ago and yet it was as if he'd been waiting for her all his life. She was the one who made him laugh, made him dance. Made him want to sing.

Walking through the quiet streets, he should have been concentrating on the future, plans that had been a year in the making. Instead it was Diana Metcalfe who filled his head, heated him to the heart, made nightingales sing in the heart of London.

* * *

Her father was dozing in front of the television, not conspicuously waiting for his little girl to come home, but he never went to bed until he knew she was safely in. As a teenager it had driven her mad. It still did but, a mother herself, these days Diana understood the need to know that your family was safe before you could rest.

'Busy day?' he asked.

'Above average,' she said, managing a grin as she peeled off her jacket. 'An outbreak of food poisoning meant that I had the number one car and a sheikh.' About whom the least said the better. Her father could read her like a book. 'Did you manage okay?' she asked, by way of diversion. 'Freddy wasn't too much for you?'

'He was as good as gold. He's spark out, bless him.' He eased himself to his feet, limped into the kitchen, turning on the tap with his left hand, then holding the kettle beneath it. She wanted to say, Sit down…let me… but understood that his self-esteem was involved. Knew that the more he did, the better it was for his mobility. Her need, his determination, to look after Freddy for her had done more for his recovery from the stroke than all the months of phsyio. Had given him a reason to push himself to be mobile. 'What'll you have? Tea, chocolate?'

All she wanted was to get to her room, shut the door, be on her own so that she could unravel the emotional tangle she'd got herself in, get her head around it, but her father looked forward to hearing about her day. 'Chocolate, if you'll have some with me. Has Mum gone up?'

'Hours ago. She was rushed off her feet at the shop today, doing the flowers for some fancy society wedding. She looked whacked out.'

'She could do with a holiday,' Diana said, trying not to envy all those journalists and tour operators, being whisked away, first class on Sheikh Zahir's magic carpet. 'Maybe we could all go somewhere when school breaks up.'

'You should be going on holiday with people your own age,' he said, then looked away.

'I don't think Freddy would fit in with an eighteen-thirty package, do you?' she joked, pretending she hadn't noticed.

'We'd look after him. You need to get out more. Get a life.'

'Freddy is my life,' she said.

'Di—'

'How's the Test Match going?' she asked.

Once launched on the safer subject of cricket, her father's passion, all she had to do was say 'absolutely' in all the appropriate places while he gave her chapter and verse on the weaknesses in the England team, the poor eyesight of the umpires, the quality of the wicket, while she drank her chocolate.

Then, having rinsed her mug, she dropped a kiss on his balding head.

'Tell Mum that I'll see to Freddy in the morning. I don't have to go in until nine. Don't stay up too late,' she chided, playing up to the pretence that he'd stayed up to watch something he wanted to see on the television, rather than because he was waiting for her to come home.

She looked in on Freddy, straightened the cover that had slipped from his shoulders, lightly touching his dark curls. Five years old and already a heart-breaker, just like the man who'd fathered him.

'Night, angel,' she murmured, picking up the snowstorm that sat on his bookshelf. The snow-flakes stirred, but she didn't shake it, just returned it to its place. 'Sleep tight.'

Safe in her own room, she sat on the bed, opened the drawer of her night table and took out the little box in which she kept her treasures. At the bottom was a photograph taken at a party. Just a bunch of people turning as someone had called out 'smile'. It was mere chance that she'd been on the same picture as Pete O'Hanlon, that someone had given it to her.

All she had of Freddy's father.

The only reason she kept it was because, one day, Freddy would insist on knowing who his father was. By then, hopefully, memories, like the photograph, would have faded, people would have moved away and his name would have been forgotten. And Freddy would be valued for himself as a decent young man.

The only reason she looked at it now was because five years had, without her noticing it, dulled her sense of danger. Because she needed to remind herself how much damage falling in lust could do.

Eventually she closed the box, put it away. Hung up her uniform, laid out a clean shirt and underwear for the morning. Brushed her teeth. Finally crawled into the same single bed that she'd slept in all her life. And discovered that she'd been working on the wrong memory because the moment she closed her eyes she was confronted with Sheikh Zahir's smile.

The one that barely showed on the surface, was no more than a warmth behind his eyes.

Felt his long fingers cradling her head, the touch of his breath on her cheek, his mouth…

Diana finally dropped off, but her sleep was disturbed by dreams in which she was driving a sparkly pink taxi around and around the inside a snow globe. She was constantly being hailed by Sheikh Zahir who, when she stopped, didn't get in the back but just looked at her and said, 'Kiss me, I'm a prince.'

Then, when she did, he turned into a frog.

She woke with a start, her heart pounding, her mouth dry, for a moment unsure where she was.

The low, insistent peeping of the alarm finally

broke through the fug of sleep and, with a groan, she killed the sound, rolled over and got out of bed in one movement. It was still early and her eyes were heavy, but she didn't want to risk closing them and having that dream start up again.

Pulling on her dressing gown, she went across the landing to Freddy's room to be there, as promised, when he woke and give her mother an extra half an hour in bed. Make the most of the luxury of an unusually late start since she wasn't due to pick up Zahir from the hotel until ten o'clock.

Assuming, of course, that Jack was still laid low.

Say what she liked about him, Jack Lumley wouldn't malinger; he'd be back at work today if it was humanly possible. Or even if it wasn't. Inspecting his precious car for the slightest mark, the smallest bit of dust and heaven help her if he found any.

Let him look.

He'd never be able to tell his car had been out of the yard. Well, not unless he tried to sit in it. She'd had to pull the seat forward to accommodate her shorter legs and hadn't thought to put it back.

'Bad girl, Diana,' she said, grinning as she gave her wrist a light tap. 'Write out one hundred times, "I must always return the seat to its original position."'

'Mummy?'

Freddy blinked, then, wide awake in an instant, bounced out of bed, grabbing his 'good work' sticker and holding it up for her to see.

'Look!'

'Shh…' she said, putting her finger to her lips. 'It's early. Don't wake Grandma and Grandpa.'

'Look, Mummy!' he whispered, holding it right in front of her face.

'Terrific!' she whispered back, scooping him up and carrying him downstairs, treasuring this precious time when, for once, she could share breakfast with him, watch over him as he cleaned his teeth. Walk him to school so that her mother wouldn't have to go out of her way but could go straight to the bus stop.

Her dad was right, she thought, as all three of them muddled together in the hall, gathering their belongings, making sure that Freddy had everything he needed for the day, her mother was looking tired and, on an impulse, she gave her a hug.

'What's that for?' she demanded in her don't-be-daft voice.

'Nothing. Everything.' Then, sideswiped by the unexpected sting of tears, she turned quickly away, calling back to her father in the kitchen, 'I'll give you a call later, Dad, let you know what's happening.'

'Don't worry about us,' he said, coming to the door. 'I'll be waiting when Freddy comes out of school. Maybe we'll have a look at the river, eh? What do you say, son?'

'Can we?' Freddy's face lit up and, smiling at her dad, Diana reached for her little boy's hand.

Her mother coughed meaningfully, shaking her head. Then, 'You don't have to walk all the way to the gate. I leave him at the corner and he walks the rest of the way all by himself.'

'He does?' she squeaked. Then, doing her best to smile, 'You do?'

Freddy nodded.

'I watch him every step of the way,' her mother mouthed in silent reassurance.

'Well…' it was only a few steps from the corner to the school gate, but Diana still had to swallow hard '…that is grown up!'

Her little boy was growing up much too fast. Making giant leaps while she was too busy working to notice. To be a full-time mother.

But what choice did she have if she was going to make a life for him? She couldn't rely on her parents for ever. She'd put them through so much already. Could never quite get away from the fear that she'd caused her father's stroke.

'Don't forget that you've got parents' evening tonight,' her dad called after her.

'It's engraved in my brain,' she promised, turning to wave from the gate.

At the corner nearest to the school she managed to restrain herself from kissing Freddy, stuffing her hands into her pockets so that she wouldn't be tempted to do anything as embarrassing as wave. Watched him as he ran away from her and was swallowed up by the mass of children in the playground and waited to make sure that he was absorbed, accepted.

Why wouldn't he be?

Half the children in his class were living in one parent families. But at least most of them had a father—even if an absent one—somewhere.

She turned and, blinking furiously, walked quickly down the road to the Capitol Cars garage.

Zahir had not slept.

He and James had worked through most of the night, putting the finishing touches to details that had been a year in the planning.

It wasn't lack of sleep that blackened his early morning mood, however, but an email from Atiya, his youngest sister.

She'd written, full of excitement, about his forth-coming wedding, eager to let him know what she thought of each of the bridal prospects on their mother's 'shortlist', which was awaiting his return. Since Atiya knew them all and was evidently thrilled to the core at the prospect of him marrying one of her dearest friends, she had taken immense pleasure in describing each of them in detail so that he would have something other than their mother's opinion—what, after all, did mothers know?—on which to make his choice.

This one, apparently, had beautiful hair. That one a stunning figure. A third wasn't so pretty but had the loveliest smile and a truly sweet nature.

It had, he thought, all the charm of a cattle show, with him as the prize bull. It was, however, a timely reminder of who he was. What was expected of him.

Which did not include dancing in the street with his enchanting chauffeur.

CHAPTER FIVE

'DI…'

Sadie had been waiting for her and she crossed to the office, assuming that the summons heralded a return to normal and trying to be glad. Sheikh Zahir had no doubt regretted his impulse to kiss her, dance with her—fooling around with the 'help' was always a mistake—and conceded that James Pierce might have had a point. Given him the go-ahead to call Sadie and arrange for another driver.

Which, or so the small inner voice of reason assured her, was a very good thing. She was still fighting off the memory of that dream. It would save embarrassment all round.

She just wished her inner voice could sound more convincing. But then her inner voice hadn't felt the power of that final look, a connection that went soul deep…

'What's the plan, boss?' she asked with determined brightness. 'Back to normal is it? You should have phoned, I could have come in earlier.'

Sadie shook her head. 'I've got someone in to cover the minibus for the rest of the week. Jack is still *hors de combat* and, while he's promising he'll be in tomorrow, I can't see him being fit for anything but local jobs until next week. Are you going to be okay for another late one?'

Zahir hadn't pulled the plug?

The fact the brightness was no longer forced, but blindingly genuine, warned her that she was playing with fire. But it was so long since she'd been warm…

'How late? Freddy has a parents' evening at school this evening.'

'Well, let's see. Sheikh Zahir has to be back in London by six so, if you could handle that part of his day, I can find someone to cover the evening.'

'No problem, then.'

'Apparently not. I'll give you a call later to let you know who it is so that you keep Sheikh Zahir in the picture. And I'll write you in for the rest of this job.'

Diana swallowed. 'Thank you, Sadie. I appreciate your confidence.' Maybe, today, she'd live up to it.

Sadie, oblivious, smiled. 'You've earned it. Enjoy your day at the seaside.'

'The seaside?'

Sadie handed over the paperwork. 'Sheikh Zahir is visiting a boatyard and marina, apparently.'

'Really?' Obviously her idea of non-stop work and Sheikh Zahir's idea of it did not coincide. 'Well, great,' she said, taking the worksheet to check out where they were going, wishing it was Freddy she was taking for a day on the beach. Somehow she couldn't see James Pierce taking off his shoes, rolling up his trouser legs and going for a paddle.

Zahir, on the other hand...

She refused to go with that image. *No more of that, my girl, she told herself. Behave yourself. Just concentrate on all the extra hours it will mean.* The extra money. She might be able to manage something a bit special for her and Freddy in the half-term holiday. A short break at Disney-land Paris, perhaps, if she was lucky enough to grab a cheap last-minute deal.

Or maybe she'd be better advised putting the money in her savings account for his future. Except, of course that children didn't understand the concept of the 'future'. For them there was only *now*.

'Okay?' Sadie asked, when she didn't move.

'Fine. I was just wondering if you wanted me to bring you back a stick of rock,' she joked.

'I'll pass, thanks,' Sadie said with a grin. 'Besides, I doubt the kind of marina that a sheikh would patronize has much call for bright pink candy, do you?'

A timely reminder, should she need one, that he lived in a different world from the one she'd been born into. A reminder she'd do well to keep front and centre next time he looked at her. Smiled at her. Murmured something in that seductive voice.

Maybe she should invest in a pair of earplugs…

Sheikh Zahir was standing on the footpath talking to James Pierce when she pulled in to the front of the hotel three minutes before ten.

He was dressed casually in a cream linen jacket, softly pleated chinos, a dark brown band-collar shirt left open at the neck, with a slim leather document case hanging loosely from one hand. James Pierce, on the other hand, was giving no quarter to a day by the sea. He was dressed in a pinstripe suit with a sober silk tie—full city-slicker gear—with the laptop which never seemed to leave his side clamped firmly in his fist.

She groaned.

James Pierce had had it in for her from the moment he'd set eyes on her and would no doubt have some sarcastic remark all lined up to deliver on the subject of having been kept waiting; she was sure the fact that *they* were early would cut no ice with him.

He'd grumbled about being kept waiting last night; anyone would think she'd loitered, had stopped for a burger or something, instead of taking a straight there-and-back run from Mayfair.

But as Zahir caught sight of her—no smile of any kind—he said something to the other man, then, as Top Hat opened the door, stepped into the back of the car.

Alone.

James Pierce, having taken a moment to give her what could only be described as a 'look'—what *was* his problem?—turned and walked back into the hotel.

Which meant that they were going to spend the entire day alone together?

Be careful what you wish for…

'In your own time, Metcalfe,' Zahir said, when she didn't immediately pull away.

'Isn't Mr Pierce coming with us?' she asked a touch desperately.

'He can't spare the time. He has contracts, leases to sign. A lawyer's work is never done.' Unable to help herself, she checked the mirror. He was waiting for her, his look thoughtful. 'Disappointed, Metcalfe? Did you manage to break the ice and make friends when you picked him up last night?'

'We didn't dance, if that's what you mean,' she said. So much for keeping her distance. Being professional. 'I didn't want to drive off and leave him if he'd just gone back inside to collect something he'd forgotten,' she said in an attempt to retrieve the situation.

'Forgotten?' Zahir marginally raised a single brow. 'Are you suggesting that he's fallible?'

'Oh… No…'

Too late she realised that he was being ironic.

Oh, Lord…

She pulled out into Park Lane, glad of the turmoil of the London traffic to keep her occupied, not that there were any further distractions from the rear of the car.

Sheikh Zahir, having teased her once, presumably in repayment for that 'dancing' remark, was apparently too absorbed by the paperwork he'd brought with him to bother once they were on their way.

Which should have been a relief.

But it was like waiting for the other shoe to drop.

First her shoulder muscles began to tighten up, then her neck stiffened with the effort of keeping her mouth shut. Would music disturb him?

She glanced in the mirror, saw that he was deep in concentration. Had, apparently, forgotten she was there. An example she'd do well to follow.

Zahir stared at the papers in front of him, doing his best to concentrate on the figures, trying not to think about the woman in front of him, the nape of her neck exposed by hair swept up under her cap. Hair that even now was escaping in soft tendrils that brushed against her pale skin.

Trying not to think about how that hair, that skin had felt against his hand. The way his hand had nestled so neatly into her waist. How her fingers had felt against his lips.

His sister's email, annoying though it had been, had brought him firmly back to earth and he was resolute in his determination that this charming but, ultimately, foolish flirtation he'd begun without a thought for the consequences must go no further. Diana Metcalfe deserved better from him.

His family deserved better from him.

Today, he reminded himself, was all about the marina at Nadira Creek.

Lunch at the local yacht club with the CEO of the chandlery with whom he was negotiating a contract to run the dockside services for him. Then a tour of the Sweethaven Marina to take a look at the facilities offered at the top end of the business, which would also give him a chance to check out the latest in state-of-the-art sailing dinghies, diving equipment, windsurfers.

Last, but definitely not least, a visit to the boatyard to look at the yacht he'd commissioned more than a year ago and was now ready for his pre-delivery inspection.

And that was the only indulgence he would permit himself on this trip; the silk finish of polished mahogany and gleaming brass were a great deal safer than the touch of soft ivory skin. Warm lips.

Finalising the details of a contract was considerably less dangerous than teasing Diana Metcalfe in the hope of another glimpse of an errant dimple that appeared at the corner of her mouth when she was battling not to smile. And losing.

Safer all round than provoking her into forgetting to be polite, to just be herself. And then kissing her. Waltzing her along London streets…

He took out the folder detailing the management fees, working through the list of queries James had detailed, equally firm in his resolve not to catch her eye in the mirror.

Not to ask about her family. Why it was her father 'used' to sing to her mother. And, presumably, didn't now. Her life.

Ask her why, when she wasn't smiling, she sometimes looked a little…lost.

Diana checked the mirror as she approached a roundabout, joined the motorway. Sheikh Zahir was working, concentrating on the file he was holding, and yet she had the strongest feeling that, a split second before she'd glanced up, he'd been looking not at his papers, but at her, waiting for that moment when she'd checked the mirror, met his gaze.

Or maybe that was what she wanted to believe.

She was clearly going crazy.

It wasn't that she doubted his readiness to flirt; he'd already proved himself to be world class in the subject and she'd promised herself that today she wouldn't be drawn in, but keep her cool. Be a professional. Not because she knew James Pierce would rat on her to Sadie in a heartbeat if he suspected she'd stepped over some invisible, but definite, line in the sand. No matter how great the temptation. And she had been tempted; admitting to it made resistance easier.

Not because of her job, but because, to Sheikh Zahir, it would be no more than a diversion.

Probably.

No! Absolutely.

Utterly meaningless.

In which case, why would he think twice about snagging her attention? If it meant nothing, he'd do it. Wouldn't he?

Oh, get a grip, Di! Why on earth would a man with a stunningly beautiful princess hanging off his arm even look at you?

Good question. He had looked, looked again and then he'd touched, danced…

Maybe he couldn't help himself. If the newspapers were anything to go by, powerful men often couldn't. Help themselves. And power was, or so she'd heard, an aphrodisiac. Women probably threw themselves at him all the time. Maybe he considered her, as his female driver, to be fair game. A perk of the job.

A little squeak of distress escaped her and she caught a movement in the mirror as he looked up. Then, after a moment, looked away.

No. That was wrong.

Zahir wasn't like that.

He hadn't kissed her like that.

It hadn't been a grope. It had been the sweetest kiss. And if he'd expected more, he would never have left her last night, walked away.

Nevertheless, she took her sunglasses from the dashboard, flicked them open and put them on. A personal safety barrier against further eye-contact in the mirror, accidental or not.

A long, silent hour later, she pulled into the car park on the quay at Sweethaven, once a small fishing port but now the playground for well-heeled yachting types with all the money in the world to indulge their passion.

Tucked into folds of the Downs, where the river widened into an estuary before running into the sea, the small, picture-perfect town was well served with expensive shops and attractive restaurants.

The whole place positively shouted money; or was that the sound of ropes, or sheets, or whatever they were called, clanging against the masts of the flotilla of expensive yachts moored in the marina?

She opened the rear door while her passenger was still stuffing papers into his document case. Stepping out of the car, he handed it to her.

'Come with me, Metcalfe.'

What?

'Um…'

He glanced back. 'Lose the hat.'

Her hand flew, in a protective gesture, to her head.

'You don't like it?' she demanded, completely forgetting her determination to keep her lip buttoned. Or that she loathed the thing herself.

Drawing attention to herself was a mistake. He stopped, turned, taking a slow tour of her appearance, from sensible shoes, via trousers cut for comfort, a slightly fitted collarless jacket that was cut short above her hips until, finally, his gaze came to rest on that hat.

'I don't like anything you're wearing. Be grateful it's only the hat I want you to take off.'

For a moment she stood open-mouthed, but he'd already turned away and was walking towards a two-storey stone building with a sign that read 'Sweethaven Yacht Club'.

Who was that?

And what had he done with the Sheikh Zahir she'd danced with last night?

To think she'd been giving him the benefit of…

'Grateful!' She tossed the hat, along with her driving gloves, into the car. Then, on an impulse, she unbuttoned her jacket and added it to the pile and pulled out one of Capitol's burgundy sweatshirts that she'd stowed in case of emergencies—you wouldn't want to change a wheel in your best uniform jacket—and knotted it around her shoulders. Pulled a face at her reflection in the wing mirror. 'At least the man has taste.'

There was, she reminded herself, the beautiful princess as prima facie evidence of the fact. Which was maybe why, having removed her jacket, she clung to the safety barrier of the sunglasses. She pushed them firmly up her nose, locked the car and, taking a deep breath, tucked the folder under her arm and went after him.

Zahir, having reached the safe haven of the yacht club's entrance lobby, stopped to gather himself.

He could not believe he'd said that. Had no excuse, other than the build-up of tension, seeing Diana so close, knowing that she was out of reach.

When she'd done that not-quite-meeting-his-eyes thing, something inside him had snapped and, knowing that an invitation wouldn't bring her to him, he'd made it an order. And then had made a remark so blatantly personal that her shock had been palpable.

Maybe that was the answer, he thought, as he eased his shoulders. Maybe, if she thought he was some kind of sexual predator, she wouldn't have to fight quite so hard to contain that tormenting little smile…

'Zahir! I saw you arrive and was beginning to think you'd forgotten the way. Come on up…'

As Diana stepped inside the yacht club, everything went suddenly dark and, with the utmost reluctance, she pushed the glasses up into her hair and looked around.

A receptionist, regarding her with a smile, said, 'They're upstairs.'

'Oh, right. Thanks.'

Upstairs proved to be not offices but a restaurant and bar where Zahir and another man, of about the same age but slighter and with his face weathered by sun and sea, were standing.

They both turned as she approached. Zahir hesitated for no more than a heartbeat as he took in her appearance, before extending a hand to draw her into their conversation.

'Metcalfe, this is Jeff Michaels. He's going to buy us lunch.'

Lunch?

Zahir didn't wait for her to protest. Didn't give her time to consider whether she wanted to protest. That was probably a good thing, since he'd put her in a situation where it was impossible for her to tell him that this was *seriously* inappropriate. At least not without making them both look stupid.

Taking full advantage of her stunned silence— probably realising that it wouldn't last—he turned to his companion and said, 'Jeff, Diana Metcalfe is one of my UK team.'

'Delighted to meet you, Diana,' he said, offering his hand as if she were a *real* person. Reacting on automatic pilot, she took it, doing her best to respond to his welcoming smile. 'Can I get you something to drink?'

Um... Um... Um...

The confusion lingered, but thankfully the gibbering 'ums' remained locked up inside her head— 'team' members did not 'um'—and, gathering herself, she said, 'Water, thanks. Still.'

Jeff nodded to the barman, glanced around at the busy bar and said, 'It'll be quieter on the terrace.' Before Zahir could answer, he turned to her, 'That's if you'll be warm enough, Diana?'

A little too warm if the truth were told, although it wasn't the ambient temperature that was heating her up but the fact that Zahir had hijacked her without so much as a by-your-leave.

What was he *thinking?*

Hadn't he learned a thing from his little moonlighting jaunt as a waiter? Food, more specifically feeding a woman, could lead a man into all kinds of temptation. Lead a woman, for that matter.

She tried not to look at him, but couldn't help herself. His face, however, offered no help, no clue to his thoughts. She'd seen him do that before, she realised, in the toy store, with a smile that was no more than a disguise. A mask to cover any hint of what he was feeling.

Then, and later when James Pierce had joined

them, he'd given her a glimpse behind the mask, had drawn her into his private world with a silent invitation to become his fellow conspirator.

There was no smile hidden in the depths of his cool grey eyes now. Even the sensuous droop of his lower lip had been jacked up into a straight line.

Whatever he was thinking, he was making damn sure no one else knew. Including her. And tempting though it was to provoke some kind of a response she very much doubted he'd be amused if she excused herself on the grounds that today she'd had the forethought to provide herself with a packed lunch.

Played the thanks-but-no-thanks, see-you-later gambit.

Instead she gave Jeff one of her best smiles and said, 'I'll be perfectly warm enough, thank you.'

'This way, then.' He lifted an avuncular arm to usher her towards the terrace, then, obviously thinking better of it, let it drop, instead leading the way to a sheltered corner.

It was one of those perfect May days, the temperature in the mid-seventies, with just enough breeze at the coast to fill the sails of a flotilla of dinghies that were making a picture postcard scene of the estuary.

'Do you sail?' Jeff asked, following her gaze.

'No.' She sat down. Then, smiling up at him, 'Never had the opportunity.'

'Hopefully you will do soon,' Jeff replied.

'As I said, Metcalfe is part of my UK team,' Zahir interposed smoothly. 'I'm in the process of setting up an office in London. If everything goes to plan, James will stay here and run it.'

'Expensive. I'd have thought it would be more cost effective to leave this end of things to specialist travel agents.'

'For the purely tourist end of the business, I agree.'

'You're expanding your business?'

'A business not expanding is a business in decline.'

'Right…'

The steward arrived with their drinks and the menu, and taking advantage of the distraction, Zahir looked across at her and their shared knowledge was like an electric spark leaping across a vacuum.

'It's just bar meals at lunchtime during the week, I'm afraid,' Jeff said, apologising to her rather than Zahir, then, apparently catching the intensity of the look that passed between them, fell silent.

'A sandwich is the most I ever eat in the middle of the day,' Diana said, filling the gap, when Zahir remained silent. 'And I don't always get that.' Then, when Jeff had gone through to the bar to place their order, she whispered urgently, 'What are you doing? Why am I here?'

For a moment she thought he wasn't going to

answer, then, with a lift of his shoulders, he said, 'To create a level playing field.'

'What?'

'I find you distracting, Metcalfe. It's not your fault—you can't help how you look—but if I'm to be distracted, it's only fair that Jeff should be similarly handicapped. It seems to be working. He can't keep his eyes off you.'

She stared at him.

In her uniform, flat shoes, absolute minimum of make-up, she was about as distracting as lukewarm soup in the middle of winter. 'What on earth are you talking about?'

He blinked slowly and without warning a hot surge of colour rushed to her cheeks. 'Oh, no…'

'You distracted me when I should have been glad-handing journalists, although I have to say that the sheer effort of keeping you out of my head gave me a real edge over dinner last night. Those bankers didn't know what had hit them.'

'You did seem a little high last night. If you don't mind me saying so.'

'Billion dollar deals tend to have that effect. Make me want to sing, to dance…'

'Zahir!'

'You see. You say my name and I can't even decide what I want for lunch. Distracting.'

'If that's the case, then it would probably be a

good thing if I left you to it and went for a walk,' she said, getting to her feet.

And he got himself another driver for tomorrow.

'Stay where you are, Diana.' Before she could open her mouth to protest, he added, 'Out of sight is not out of mind.'

'This is outrageous.' She glared at him. 'You expect me to sit here and "distract" the man, while you pull your tycoon act and take him to the cleaners?'

'Did I say that?'

'What else could you possibly mean?' she demanded. And she had the doubtful pleasure of seeing the impassive mask slip, feeling the heat from eyes that were—momentarily—anything but cool. 'You're quite mad, you know,' she said, subsiding into her chair, not in obedience to his command but because her legs refused to keep her upright. 'I'm not some *femme fatale*.'

'No?' Then, after a moment's thought, 'No.'

Dammit, he wasn't supposed to agree with her! And this was definitely not the moment for him to smile. If that lip moved, sheikh or not, he was cats' meat…

Maybe he recognised the danger because he managed to restrain himself, confine himself to an apparently careless shrug.

'In that case, why are you making such a fuss?'

CHAPTER SIX

MAKING a fool of herself, more like.

Diana swallowed but her mouth was suddenly dry and she picked up her glass with a hand that was visibly shaking and took a mouthful of water.

She'd known, right from the beginning, that Sheikh Zahir wasn't going to be a conventional passenger. He might not have lived up to her Lawrence of Arabia fantasy, but it was obvious, from the moment that boy had cannoned into him, from that first meeting of eyes through the rear-view mirror, that he was going to be trouble.

For her.

And the kind of disturbance that even now was churning beneath her waistband confirmed her worst fears.

Inappropriate? This wasn't just inappropriate. This was plain stupid and Sadie would have an absolute fit if she had the slightest idea of just how unprofessionally she had behaved right from the very beginning.

Chatting to him as if he were someone she'd met in a bus queue. Dragging him off to The Toy Warehouse and giving him the down-and-dirty gossip on the frog and princess scandal. Sharing canapés with him on a riverside bench when he should have been working the media.

Sharing an earth-shattering, world-changing kiss with a man whose 'partner' was inside the gallery, taking the strain.

All mouth, no brains, that was her.

There was absolutely no way there could be a personal connection between them other than some brief sexual dalliance which would obviously be a meaningless fling for him—and she felt a moment of pity for the beautiful princess—while it could only be damaging to her, professionally and personally. Even supposing she was the kind of woman who 'flung' around with a man who was attached, no matter how loosely, to another woman.

Who 'flung' full stop.

One fling had got her into enough trouble to last a lifetime.

And if he had anything else in mind, well he was the dumb one. He was a sheikh. She was a chauffeur. He was so far out of her orbit that he might as well be on Mars and it didn't need the brains of Einstein to figure out how that equation would work out.

It wasn't even as if she was fancy-free, at liberty

to indulge herself, take the risk, no matter how self-destructively. She had responsibilities. A five-year-old son she would always put first, not out of duty, but out of love.

Why, oh, why, couldn't her big chance have come on the day when the car had been booked to drive some grey, middle-aged executive whose only interest was the movement of the FTSE or the NASDAQ?

Someone who wouldn't even have noticed she existed.

'Tomorrow,' she began, determined to put a stop to this before one of them did something really stupid. Something that she, at least, would regret—and she already had enough of those to last her a lifetime. Before she forgot all of the above and began to believe what his eyes seemed to be saying. 'Tomorrow,' she repeated, with determination…

'Tomorrow I'm flying to Paris,' he said, cutting her short before she could tell him that tomorrow he'd have another driver. If not Jack, someone else would have to take over from her, although what on earth she'd tell Sadie…

Somehow she didn't think, 'He looked at me and I came over all *inappropriate*…' would go down at all well. She'd be lucky to keep the school run. But she'd have to take that risk. Better to lose her job than fall back into a pit it had taken her months, years, to climb out of.

'Want to come?' he said, jerking her back to the here and now.

'To Paris. With you?'

'The alternative is being at James's beck and call.'

'Oh.'

What was that about being careful what you wished for? Although, if it meant she could keep this job for another day…

'Well, great!'

He wasn't fooled for a minute. 'He's not a soft touch like me, Diana. You'd probably be advised to bring a packed lunch,' he said. And then he smiled.

Not the mask smile. Not the meaningless one that had so annoyed her when he'd used it to reduce a careless shop assistant to slavery. But the one that spoke directly to her, that said, 'We are connected, you and I. Deny it all you want, but you know the truth.'

It took her good intentions, all her common sense and heated them to dust, blew them away, leaving her momentarily struggling for breath.

'I brought a packed lunch today,' she said. 'I was going to sit on the harbour wall and share it with the seagulls.'

'Were you? Well, the day is a long way from over. Maybe we could do that later.'

We…

'It won't be long,' Jeff said, rejoining them before she could say anything. Just as well. For the second time that day she was lost for words. That had to be a record… 'Do you want to clear up any final details on the contract while we're waiting?'

'I'm really quite happy with it,' Zahir replied, 'but, Metcalfe had a few queries.' He held out his hand for the folder she'd put on the table in front of her. She handed them over without a word and Zahir extracted a single sheet of paper from the file and offered it to the other man. 'If we can iron out these few details, keep her happy, you can have your office print up the final version and I'll sign it before I leave.'

Jeff glanced at the figures, then, thoughtfully, at her. She gripped her lower lip between her teeth to keep it tightly closed.

'There's no kidding you, is there?' he said with a wry grin in her direction. 'If I conceded the first three without an argument, will you consider splitting the difference on the management fee?'

Zahir rescued her, holding up a hand as if to silence her. 'Don't be hard on the man, Diana. That's fair.' Then, offering the hand to Jeff, 'We have a deal.'

If Diana had felt any concern about Zahir's intentions, Jeff's broad smile quickly reassured her.

'I'll fly out to Nadira next week to set things in motion, Zahir,' he said. Then, turning to her, 'Will I see you there, Diana?'

She'd just picked up her glass and taken a swallow of water, so Zahir answered for her.

'I'm hoping Diana will accept my invitation to familiarize herself with the resort in the very near future. If you're there at the same time we'll be glad to repay your hospitality.'

She choked and the water took the only available exit and shot out of her nose.

Gasping, shaking her head, completely unable to speak, she leapt to her feet and rushed off in the direction of the washroom.

Now what was he playing at?

Since she had no possible way of knowing, she concentrated on the practicalities of mopping the water from the front of her shirt while she regained her breath and her composure. Took her time about refastening the unravelling mess of her hair. Groped in her pocket for lipstick and came up empty. Remembered, too late, that she'd left it in her jacket pocket. Just as well; her lips had got her into enough trouble already without drawing unnecessary attention to them.

Finally, unable to put it off any longer, she returned to the terrace, where the two men were deep in a conversation involving boats.

Zahir looked up. 'Okay?'

'Fine. Thank you,' she said primly.

His only response was one of those quiet smiles that undid all the hard work of the last five minutes. At least with regard to breathing and composure.

It was all very well saying that he'd be in Paris tomorrow—and no, she couldn't possibly go with him—but she had the rest of today to get through before then.

And no escape.

The rest of lunch, however, proved uneventful since Zahir was more interested in what Jeff had to say than in winding her up. And, like an idiot, she actually found herself missing their dangerous exchanges.

Just how stupid could one woman get?

Afterwards, the two men set off to tour the marina and it was Jeff, not Zahir, who glanced back and said, 'Can we tempt you to join us, or are you more interested in the shops than boats?'

Freddy, Diana thought, would have been in his element amongst the boats. He loved going on river trips. And that was what they'd do this half-term. A jaunt up to Greenwich on the river to look at the Cutty Sark and the Maritime Museum. They could even take a ride on a narrow boat along the Regent's Canal to the Zoo.

She realised that they were waiting for her answer.

Or had she been waiting for Zahir to add his voice to the invitation? Encourage her to join them?

'The shops have it, every time,' she replied quickly, taking the wiser course and putting as much distance between them as possible.

The way things were going, he was bound to say

something, give her one of those ironic looks that would leave her with an uncontrollable desire to push him into the harbour—and how would she explain *that* to Sadie?

'How long have I got?'

'How long do you need?' Zahir replied. Then, with a smile that suggested he knew exactly what was going on in her head, said, 'An hour should do it.'

She collected her wallet from the glove box, stuffed it into her trouser pocket and set off for the town centre. Although the possibility that she'd be able to afford anything in the small, exotic boutiques they'd passed on their way down to the quay was totally nil, she'd enjoy the window-shopping. She might be short of spare cash, but she could dream.

But Sweethaven, she discovered, had more to offer than just designer boutiques and when she saw a real old-fashioned bookshop she pushed open the door and went inside.

She browsed for something for her father. Found a paperback thriller that she knew he'd love. Then she spotted a circular stand containing the small children's books that she'd loved as a child and, as she spun it, looking for something that Freddy would enjoy, she found herself face to face with a familiar title in the fairy tale series.

She took it down, flipping through it, smiling at

the remembered pictures, including the Prince, no longer a frog but respectably buttoned up to the neck in a fancy uniform as he stood beside the astonished princess.

On an impulse she picked it up, found another with every kind of nautical knot for Freddy, before realising that time was running out and hurrying back to the quayside car park. Zahir and Jeff were already there.

'I'm sorry…' she began as Jeff shook hands with Zahir, raised a hand to her and returned to his office.

'No problem. We've only just got here. Did you find anything exciting?' Then, seeing the name on the paper carrier she was holding, 'Books?'

She'd been going to give *The Princess and the Frog* to him, just to make him laugh. Quite suddenly, it didn't seem such a bright idea. 'They're children's books,' she said.

'Oh? Whose children?'

Tell him…

Tell him and see that look? The speculative You've-got-a-kid? look. The one that says, Whoa! Easy…

While she stood there, frozen, he took the carrier from her, opened it and took out the thriller and held it up. 'This is what you give children to read?'

She snatched it from him. 'That's for my dad.'

He took another look in the bag and this time came up with the book of knots that she'd bought for Freddy. 'He's a sailor?'

'He was a taxi-driver. He had a stroke.'

That set him back. 'I'm sorry, Diana.'

'He's not an invalid.'

'But he can't drive?'

'No.'

He gave her a long measuring look, then took out the last book. And that made him smile. 'Oh, I get it. You wanted to check your version against the original.'

She shook her head. 'I was close enough, but when I saw it I thought of Ameerah,' she said, fingers crossed. 'Maybe she'd like it to go with her snow globe?'

'I'm sure she'd love it.'

'Good.' She reclaimed the bag, put the books away. 'I'll wrap it for her,' she said, tucking it beneath her seat. 'You can give it to her on Saturday.'

'Why don't you give it to her yourself?'

'She doesn't know me,' she said abruptly.

'You can remedy that while we chug down the Regent's Canal.'

She wondered if he'd be as eager for her company if she suggested she bring her five-year-old son along for the ride. The one whose father had been a villain.

'I don't think so. Are you ready to go?'

He nodded but, as she backed out of the car to open the rear door for him, she discovered that he'd walked around and opened the front passenger door.

'If I sit in the back, Jeff, who's watching us from his office window right now, might just get the impression that you're no more than my chauffeur,' he said in response to her obvious confusion. 'You wouldn't want that, would you?'

'I don't actually give a damn what he thinks,' she replied. Definitely not a response out of the perfect chauffeur's handbook, but then he wasn't the perfect client. 'But you're the boss. If you want to sit in front, then sit in front.'

'Thank you for that. I was beginning to wonder for a moment. About being the boss.'

'Making me responsible for contract negotiation must have gone to my head,' she replied, before replacing her sunglasses and sliding in beside him. Bumping shoulders as he leaned towards her as he pulled down the seat belt, so that she jumped. Smiling at her as he slid it home with a click.

He was much too close. It was more than the physical effect of his wide shoulders, overflowing the seat beside her. His *presence* was invading her space, along with some subtle male scent that made him impossible to ignore and, despite her determinedly spirited, in-your-face response, her hand was shaking as she attempted to programme the SatNav with their next destination.

Five years and she hadn't once been tempted.

Had never taken a second look at a man, no matter how gorgeous. Particularly if they were gorgeous.

Pete O'Hanlon had head-turning good looks. His only 'good' characteristic, but when you were eighteen and deep in lust you didn't see that.

Since then, she'd never felt even a twinge of that lose-your-head, forget lose-your-heart—desire that she'd read about. Had heard her girlfriends talk about. Hadn't understood it.

Not that she was taking any credit for that. Her life was complicated enough without making things even more difficult for herself. Motherhood, guilt had drained every scrap of emotion she'd had to spare. Add a full-time job and who had time?

And then…wham. Out of the blue there it was. The pumping heart, the racing pulse, something darker, more urgent, that was totally different, indescribably new, that she didn't even want to think about.

Making a pretence of double checking the address, she said, 'Do I get an explanation for what happened back there? The real reason you took me into your meeting with Jeff?'

He shook his head. 'It was—nothing.'

'Pretending that I was what? Your tame number-cruncher querying his figures? That was nothing?'

'Jeff was always going to agree to those changes—they were fair, believe me—but, since you were there I realised I could cut short the haggling.'

'Really?' The question was rhetorical. Ironic.

'Really. What man could resist flattering a pretty woman?'

'Remind me never to do business with you.'

'You wouldn't have any reason to regret it, Diana.'

Was that a proposition?

She glanced at him and then just as quickly turned away as the tremor affecting her hand raced through the rest of her body so that she had to grip the steering wheel.

It sounded horribly like one.

'I've got nothing to offer you,' she managed, 'other than entertainment value and, just once, a short cut to a signature on the dotted line.'

'Diana—'

'I hope you both had a jolly good laugh when I snorted a mouthful of water down my nose.'

'It was an interesting reaction to my invitation to visit Nadira.'

Without meaning to, she looked at him. He was not laughing. Far from it.

'*That* was an invitation?' she asked disparagingly, as she tore her gaze away from him.

'You want a gold-edged card? Sheikh Zahir al-Khatib requests the pleasure…'

'I want absolutely nothing,' she said, furious with him. Furious with herself for letting him see that she cared. 'I just want to do the job I'm paid for.'

'It's no big deal, Diana,' he said carelessly. 'There'll be spare room on the media junket.'

'Oh, right. *Now* I'm tempted.'

How dared he! How damn well dared he invite her to his fancy resort for a week of sex in the sand—including her as a tax write-off along with the freebie-demanding journalists—and say it was 'no big deal'! That she would have no reason to regret it.

Too bad that the first man she had looked at since Freddy's father was not only out of her reach, but a twenty-four carat…sheikh. Her judgement where men were concerned was still, it seemed, just as rotten…

Zahir had actually been congratulating himself on his self-control as he'd climbed out of the car on their arrival at Sweethaven.

There had been a difficult moment right at the beginning of the journey when he could have easily lost it. He only had to look at Diana Metcalfe for his mind to take off without him. But he'd got a grip, had jerked it back into line, forcing himself to concentrate on what had to be done. Ignore the possibilities of what he deeply, seriously, wanted to do…

Had managed, just about, to keep his tongue between his teeth and his head down—mostly—for nearly two hours and since, like him, Diana had, after that dangerous first exchange, taken avoiding action and hidden her expressive eyes behind dark glasses, they'd travelled from the heart of London to the coast in a silence broken only by the occasional interjection of the navigation system offering direction.

It should have made things easier but, without the oddly intimate exchanges through the rear-view mirror that were driving this unexpected, unlooked for, *impossible* connection, he'd found himself noticing other things.

The shape of her ear—small and slightly pointed at the tip.

A fine gold chain around her neck that was only visible when she leaned forward slightly to check that the road was clear at a junction.

The smooth curve of her cheek as she glanced sideways to check her wing mirrors. He'd found himself forgetting the document he was holding as he'd been captivated by the slow unwinding of a strand of hair.

It was scarcely surprising that when, on their arrival at Sweethaven he'd been confronted by her standing stiffly, almost to attention, as he'd stepped out of the car—he'd lost it so completely that he'd found himself issuing not an invitation, but an order for her to join him.

Actually, on reflection, he hadn't got that bit wrong. The order part. An invitation would never have got her. An invitation offered her a choice which she would have had the good sense to decline.

She knew, they both knew, that there was, or at least should be, a barrier—a glass wall—between them. It had shattered, not when he'd kissed her, but with that ridiculous antique snow globe.

Diana, trapped in her role, was doing her best to repair the damage and he knew that nothing other than a direct order would have brought her into the yacht club. If he'd left it at that it might, just, have been okay, but he'd had to throw in that comment about her hat... And he refused to fool himself about the reason for it.

He'd wanted to see her hair again, the way it had been last night, when she'd stood by the river with the breeze tugging strands loose from her pins. Softly curled chestnut silk that had brushed against her neck, her cheek, his hand...

And it had been downhill all the way from there.

He'd stepped way beyond anything that could be considered acceptable behaviour when she'd challenged him and first his body, and then his mouth, had bypassed his brain.

He knew it would be a mistake to look at her now.

Could not stop himself.

She was staring straight ahead, the only movement the flicker of her eyes as she checked the mirror. If he'd been bright enough to sit in the back, he could have used that to catch her attention...

But then he'd have missed this profile. Missed her

stubborn little chin, her mouth set firm, almost as if she were fighting to keep it shut. There was not a sign of that sweet dimple, just a flush to her cheeks that gave a whole new meaning to the old 'you look magnificent when you're angry' cliché.

The strange thing was, he couldn't remember ever having made a woman angry before. But then he'd never felt like this about any woman and maybe that was the point. To feel passionately, it had to matter. To her as well as to him.

Maybe that was why he was angry with himself. He didn't do this. Had never, in all his thirty years, lost his head over a woman, no matter how beautiful, elegant, clever. His detachment—and theirs—had been a safety net, an acknowledgement that no matter how enjoyable the relationship, it was superficial, fleeting. Because, even though he'd deferred the inevitable, putting it off for as long as possible, he'd always known that his future was, as his cousin had suggested, written.

That his choice of bride was not his alone, but part of a tradition that went back through the ages as a way of strengthening tribal bonds.

His head understood, accepted that kind of power-broking, but then he'd walked out of the airport into the sunlight of a May morning and, in an instant, or so it seemed now, he'd been possessed by a girl who had nothing to commend her but an hourglass figure, a dimple and a total inability to keep her mouth shut.

And it was that mouth, her complete lack of control over it, rather than her luscious figure, that had hooked his attention. Had somehow enchanted him.

Diana slowed, signalled, turned into the boatyard. Gravel crunched beneath the tyres for a moment and then she drew up in the lee of a boathouse and the silence returned.

She made no move to get out, open the door for him, but remained with her hands on the wheel, looking straight ahead. He unclipped his seatbelt, half turned towards her and when that didn't get her attention either, he said, 'I'm sorry.'

He found the rarely used words unexpectedly easy to say. Maybe because he meant them. He *was* sorry. Wished he could start the day over. Start from where they'd left off last night.

If it hadn't been for that damned email, reminding him that, while he'd escaped one future, there were some duties he could not escape…

Diana's breath caught on a little sigh, her lips softened, but still she didn't look at him, still held herself aloof, at a distance.

'If I promise that I will never embarrass you in that way again, do you think you might just deign to come down off your high horse and talk to me?'

'High horse!' She swung round and glared at him. 'I'm not on any high horse!'

Indignant was better than silent. Indignant, her eyes flashed green. Indignant might so easily spill over into laughter. She laughed so easily. Made him want to laugh as no woman ever had...

'Eighteen hands at the very least,' he said, pushing it.

She shrugged, spread her hands in an 'and that means?' gesture.

He responded by raising a hand above his shoulder.

She swallowed. 'Good grief, we're talking carthorse, here.' Then, when he didn't respond with anything more than a twitch of his eyebrows, 'I might—*might*—just admit to a slightly overgrown Shetland pony.'

'One of those small, plump creatures with the uncontrollable manes?' he enquired, encouraged by the fleeting appearance of that dimple.

'They're the ones,' she admitted, doing her best to swallow down the smile that was trying very hard to break through. Then, having, against all the odds, succeeded, she added, 'Much more my style than some long-legged thoroughbred, wouldn't you say?'

'A perfect match,' he said.

For once she had no swift comeback and for the

longest moment they just looked at each other, neither of them saying a word. But smiling was the furthest thing from either of their minds.

CHAPTER SEVEN

'DON'T you have an appointment to keep?'

It was Diana, not him, who finally broke the silence after what might have been an age, but was nowhere near long enough.

'Nothing involving money.' Zahir fought down the temptation to reach out, touch his fingers to her lips to silence her so that they could return to that moment of perfect understanding. Instead, he went for a wry smile. 'I'll rephrase that. It involves a great deal of money, but the negotiations were done and dusted months ago. I'm here to take possession of the finished article.'

'Which, since we're in a boatyard, I'm guessing would be a boat?' she said, looking around her at the vast boat-building sheds, the craft pulled out of the water and propped up in cradles awaiting work.

'Got it in one and you know how it is with a new toy. It's no fun unless you can show it off to someone.'

Her gaze returned to him. It was direct, straightforward. Honest. She might blush like a girl, but there was none of that irritating coyness about her. She was direct in her look, direct in every way. Even as she acknowledged the truth of his remark with the smallest tilt of her head, she said, 'Am I the best you can do?'

He sensed more than simple bafflement that he'd choose to display his latest acquisition to his chauffeur. Suspected that her question was loaded, but he played along, turning to look in the back of the car.

'I can't see anyone else. Of course, if you would really prefer to stay here and feed the seagulls?'

Diana knew that feeding the seagulls was the safe option. The sensible option. But, for some reason, she wasn't doing sensible this week.

If she had been, she'd have politely accepted Zahir's apology and left it at that. Too late now, but then their relationship had gone far beyond politeness. Beyond the point at which she could pretend that she was just his chauffeur and use the car as her defence. The fact that he'd asked, rather than ordered only underlined that point.

He was learning.

Pity she couldn't do the same, she thought, as she opened the car door and stepped out, catching her breath as the breeze whipped at her hair.

At the marina, the sea, sheltered in the narrow estuary that the river had carved through the hills and coralled by wooden landing stages, had seemed deceptively tame.

Here the sea was a live thing, constantly on the move as it slapped against the concrete slipway, sucked at the shingle. Even the air tasted of salt.

She turned to Zahir, who was standing beside the car, waiting.

Tall, dark and so dangerous that he should have, *Warning! Close Contact With This Man Can Seriously Damage Your Peace of Mind!* stamped on his forehead.

The fact that he'd been able to tease her out of her strop the moment he'd put his mind to it was ample demonstration of the danger she was in. How would she ever be able to resist him if he really made an effort?

If he wanted more than a kiss…

She shook her head, recognising somewhere, deep inside her where she refused to go, that his apology had been a rare thing. That he had been making a very special effort.

That resistance was imperative. And, taking a slow calming breath, she turned to face him.

'If you wanted to show off your new toy,' she asked, 'why didn't you bring the Princess with you?'

'Princess?'

He was good. He really looked as if he didn't know what, who, she was talking about.

'Tall,' she prompted, holding her hand several inches above her own pitiful height. 'Blonde.' She couldn't quite bring herself to say *beautiful*. 'Your partner, according to James Pierce?'

He leaned back, his brows drawn down in a puzzled frown. 'Do you mean Lucy?'

'I don't know. How many tall, blonde partners do you have?' she snapped, angry that he wouldn't just own up, tell her the truth. That while he was flirting with her, kissing her, dancing with her, he had a thoroughbred filly at home in the stable.

Angry with herself for allowing him to waltz away with her, when she knew…

'You were talking to her when I returned the tray. If that helps,' she prompted. 'She was wearing a pale grey…'

'I'm with you,' he said, getting the picture. 'But calling her my partner is stretching it a bit.'

'Surely you are or you aren't,' she said, hating him for not being honest with her. Hating herself for caring…

'It's not like that.'

'No? What is it like, Zahir?'

'What is it like?'

His long look left her in no doubt that she'd exposed herself, had revealed feelings that would have been better kept hidden and, damn it, she was really good at 'hidden'. She could keep a secret better than anyone she knew. She'd had years of practice…

'It doesn't matter,' she said, turning away, but he stopped her. All it took was a touch to her shoulder.

'It's like this, Diana.'

And she turned back. Forget the way he looked, the way he smiled so that she felt like the only person in the world. Who could resist that low, seductively accented voice as it wrapped itself around her, warming everything within her that was vital, female, bringing it to life?

Who could resist it, when she'd been dead inside for so long?

'Really—'

She made one more effort, but he raised a hand, demanding that she listen.

'Lucy—charming, beautiful Lucy—' she flinched at each word '—was the joint owner of one of those desert tour outfits. It was poorly managed, under-capitalised, going nowhere. And the man who ran it had been arrested for fraud, amongst other things.'

His mouth tightened as if just thinking about it made him angry and suddenly she was listening.

'My cousin, Hanif—Ameerah's father—knew that I was more interested in business than diplomacy and he encouraged me to step in, take it over, see if I could make something of it. I raised the capital— it didn't take much—but when I bought Lucy out I insisted she keep a small equity in the business.' He managed a wry smile. 'Just in case I was as good as I thought I was. She'd had a raw deal.'

'What a Galahad!'

'You don't understand.' He lifted a hand as if asking her to at least try. 'But then why should you?'

'I never will unless you tell me. Not that it's any of my business,' she added, realising, somewhat belatedly, that haranguing a client about business affairs was probably not an entirely wise move. Except that she'd stopped treating Zahir like a client from, well, the moment she'd picked up the shattered snow globe.

But the admission earned her another of those smiles—the real ones—so that was okay.

'Don't go all polite on me, Diana.'

Or maybe not.

'I'm listening,' she said.

He leaned back against the car, folded him arms, looked down, as if dredging deep for what he was about to tell her. 'The men in my family are diplomats. My grandfather before he became ruler. My father, uncles, cousins. I wanted something different. Like you, I had a dream.'

'Your own airline?'

'Not quite. It takes time to learn to dream on that scale. You have to start small, then, as your imagination grows, let the dreams grow until they are big enough to fill all the available space.' He glanced up at her. 'I got my chance because Lucy's life had fallen apart. I owed her. She uses her share of the profits to fund a charity she founded, which is why she turns out for the PR stuff, as she did last night, whenever Hanif can spare her.'

Hanif…

'Your cousin,' she said, finally working out where all this was going. 'Ameerah's father.'

'And Lucy's husband.'

Diana struggled to say something to cover her stupidity but for once words failed her and all she could manage was a stumbling, 'I…um…'

Oh…sheikh!

Zahir saw her difficulty. But then he'd seen everything. That was why he'd taken the long route to make his point when he could just as easily have said, *She's my partner, but she's also my cousin's wife.*

'That wasn't the kind of partnership you were talking about was it.' he asked very softly.

A hole in the ground, opening up to swallow her whole, would be welcome right now, she decided as, left with no place to hide, she shook her head.

'Whatever made you think—?'

'I saw her last night when I returned the tray,' she cut in quickly, before he reminded her exactly what she'd been thinking. 'You were together. You looked so close and when he saw me looking Mr Pierce told me that she was your partner. I thought…' She dismissed what she'd thought with an awkward, mean-ingless gesture.

'A simple misunderstanding.'

She didn't think so.

'*His partner*…' The way James Pierce had said it had been full of meaning. He'd meant her to believe…

No. That was ridiculous. Much more likely her imagination, working overtime, leaping to conclu-sions when she'd seen him standing so close to a beautiful woman just minutes after he'd kissed her.

Good grief, she must have it bad if she'd let her imagination run so *green*. She must really have it bad if she felt this good knowing that it wasn't true.

While she was still trying to find words that would not betray her as a complete idiot—a jealous idiot at that—he rescued her, making a gesture in the direction of boatyard.

'Actually, you're right, Lucy would have loved the chance to see the yacht. In fact she's calling in every favour I owe her in return for the right to give it a test run as a wedding anniversary gift to Hanif before it's chartered to the public.'

'You're going to charter it?' Diana asked, grabbing for the impersonal in an attempt to distract him from the fact that she'd just betrayed feelings that were just plain…*inappropriate*!

'I could not justify the expense for my own personal use. Even if I had the time. But today it is all mine.'

And, with the slightest of bows, he offered her his hand. 'In the absence of Princess Lucy al-Khatib, Miss Metcalfe, will you do me the immense honour of allowing me to share this moment with you?'

He had never treated her as if she were just his chauffeur, but at this moment she recognised that he was treating her like a princess and she laid her hand against his.

He closed his hand over hers, tucked it beneath his arm and, heading for the boatyard office, said, 'My plan is to use the yacht as part of a wedding package. I'd value your opinion on that.'

'I don't think I'm your natural market, Zahir.'

He glanced at her. 'Are you telling me that you don't dream?'

'Not at all. It's just that my dreams are confined to pink taxis.' And a prince who turns into a frog. The only way this could turn out. But it was her Cinderella moment and she was going to make the most of it.

'There's nothing wrong with the pink taxi dream, but maybe I can broaden your horizons.'

'To what? A pink yacht?'

'Just wait until you see her,' he said, with a sudden smile that betrayed an oddly boyish enthusiasm. 'There's a very small island in Nadira Creek that is going to make a perfect wedding venue. I'm building a restaurant there, with a traditional wind tower to draw the air down over a basement pool to cool it naturally. A pavilion for romantic Westerners to make their vows.'

'It's just for tourists, then?'

'An Arab wedding traditionally takes place at the bride's home…' He shook his head. 'At Nadira, after the ceremony, the feasting, the yacht will be waiting to carry the honeymooners away, leaving the world behind…'

He left the rest to her already overcharged imagination.

'It sounds enchanting,' she said, concentrating very hard not to go there. 'And expensive.' Then, 'But very romantic.'

'It will be.'

'Which?'

'All three,' he assured her. And the boyish smile faded, leaving only a very adult warmth in his eyes.

The yacht certainly looked expensive. White, sleek, beautiful, and so much larger than she'd anticipated, that Diana almost succumbed to another '…*oh, sheikh…*' moment.

'You'd probably like to look around the accommodation, miss,' the boat builder suggested, 'while I show Sheikh Zahir the engines?'

Zahir hesitated, then, turning to follow the man below to inspect powerful engines that were, even now, sending a quiet hum through the yacht, he said, 'Go where you like, Diana. I'll catch up with you.'

She suspected that she knew at least as much about engines as Zahir. From the time she could reach inside the bonnet of his taxi, she'd been asking questions and her father had taught her all he knew, even as he'd taught her to drive on private roads, so that she'd passed her driving test only days after her seventeenth birthday.

But men were funny about stuff like that, so she did as she was told and wandered over the yacht, marvelling over the ingenuity of the fittings in the galley, sighing over the minimalist luxury of the accommodation. Coming to a halt when she opened the door to the main stateroom which, dominated by a huge bed, half hidden by rich silk drapes, was quite clearly the honeymoon suite. Zahir had certainly widened the horizons of her dreams she thought, as her imagination ran amok…

Definitely time for some fresh air, she decided, heading back to the deck. But the honeymoon image lingered and, as she stood in the prow, her dreams knew no bounds. A tropical sun dipping into the sea, the arm of a man who loved her around her waist, her head against his shoulder.

She shook her head to clear it.

Forget the yacht, the sunset. Only the man was important and she'd be wise to forget him too.

Everything she had, everything she could be, was down to her alone and on an impulse, she leaned forward, stretching out her arms like the heroine in the film *Titanic* and, in the absence of her own hero, telling herself that she could do anything, be anything, if only she had the courage...

Zahir dutifully stood over the glistening pistons as the engines were turned over because, as an owner taking possession, that was what was expected of him. Doing his duty when he'd far rather have stayed with Diana, wanting to see her face as he revealed his new toy to her. As he opened the door and she saw the stateroom. Certain that her reaction would tell him everything he wanted to know.

Perhaps it was as well he'd been distracted.

Better not to know...

When, finally, he could escape, he found her not below, exploring, but standing in the bow of the yacht, her arms outstretched like some figurehead... No... It was something else. A scene from a film.

She was dreaming after all and, smiling, he came up behind her, took hold of her waist and said, 'Do it properly. Step up on the rail.' Her response was to take a step back, drop her arms, but he urged her to go for it. Lifting her, he said, 'Reach for it, Diana. Reach for what you want most.'

'Zahir!'

His name was a wail of embarrassment, but he refused to listen.

'Trust me… I won't let you fall.'

Diana, feeling utterly foolish at being caught out play-acting this way, for a moment resisted, but his hands were strong, his support real, and suddenly she was there, leaning far out over the water, her eyes closed, arms stretched wide, reaching for her future as he leaned with her, his arms beneath hers, keeping her safe.

'I can feel the wind in my face,' she said, laughing, feeling like the girl she'd never been. And at her back she could feel Zahir's strength as he held her, the slight roughness of his chin against her neck, the warmth of his body quickening her to a womanhood she'd never known.

The thudding of her pulse at his closeness, an aching intimate heat, shocking in its urgency, was confirmation that life was to be seized and shaken and, for one mad moment, she came close to turning and pulling him over the edge with her, taking him with her as she plunged beneath the surface.

If they were both out of their depth they would be equal…

Except she was Cinderella and the minute they stepped off the yacht she would cease to be a princess.

'Are you sure this is a good idea?' she said shakily, backing away from the intensity of feelings that had almost overwhelmed her. Trying to keep this at a level she could handle.

She didn't do overwhelmed.

She didn't do dreams.

'It won't jinx the boat?' she persisted, when the only answer was his soft breath against her cheek.

The scene in the film had been beautiful, but the love affair, like the Titanic, had been doomed from the first reel of the movie and, in an attempt to claw herself back to reality, she opened her eyes to find that the view had changed. That they were far from the shore.

Confused, she looked down to see a lacy ripple of white where the bow broke the surface of the water.

She stared down at it for a moment, trying to work out what was happening, then, as the water moving away from her made her giddy, she pitched forward, crying out, certain she was about to fall.

But Zahir's hands were sure. He had her safe and, lifting her down, turned her so that she was facing him instead of the rush of water, drawing her close as she clung, shaking, to his shoulders, his arms around her as if he would never let her go while he murmured soft reassuring words against her hair, her temple.

She was still shaking, but not because she was afraid of falling. This wasn't fear, this was something darker, more urgent, and, as she looked up, she knew he was going to kiss her.

Not the way he'd kissed her before. This was not like that sweet, sensuous, barely there kiss.

He'd held her as he'd danced with her.

This was something else. This wasn't that light, floating touch as they'd slowly circled Berkeley Square. This was searingly close, a hungry, insistent need…

For the space of one, two, three heartbeats pounding in her ears, her head did its best to fight the seductive call to surrender, but by then her body had made a bid for independence and, overriding thought, reason, she was kissing him back.

No holds barred. No fooling. Minutes earlier she'd felt as if she were flying; this was the real thing.

Diana didn't want him to let her go. She wanted him to carry her down to that stateroom and put that incredible bed to the purpose for which it had been designed.

Maybe he would have.

Maybe, like her, he was beyond reason and in another moment they would have been beyond recall. Instead they were shocked back to reality by a sharp shower of cold water.

She jerked back, gasping for breath.

Zahir, damn him, laughed. 'Are you all right?' he asked, ignoring the water running down his face, instead wiping the spray from her cheeks with his thumbs.

'All right?' she demanded, her hair dripping down the back of her neck and trickling down inside her blouse. 'What kind of dumb question is that?'

'The "are you all right?" dumb question?' he offered.

'Fine!' she said. Beyond the fact that she'd temporarily lost her mind. That it had taken the equivalent of a bucket of cold water to bring her to her senses. 'I'm absolutely fine, if you overlook the fact that I appear to be at sea!'

'Oh, that…'

'Yes, that! Come and look at my new toy, you said. You didn't say anything about putting to sea!'

'Alan's idea,' he said. 'But running away to sea suddenly has a lot to commend it.'

She refused to answer that on the grounds that it might incriminate her.

'I'm sorry if you had a fright. Are you very wet?'

'Yes!' she said crossly. Being jerked down from that kind of high would make anyone cross. Then, more truthfully, 'No…'

'Sure? You don't want to stand around in wet clothes.'

How could she be sure of anything when she was standing this close to Zahir, her hands still clinging to his shoulders as if he were anchoring her to earth, his hands about her waist and everything in between…touching?

'Any excuse to get me out of this uniform, huh?'

Yes, well, it was the obvious next move after that mind-blowing kiss. Especially when she was clutching at his shoulders so hard that she was screwing up the linen of his jacket.

'You've got me,' he said.

And it was those three little words that brought her back to earth, to reality. He was the one thing she hadn't got. Not *him*. And she never would. Not for more than an hour or two.

That was too much like history repeating itself.

And slowly, very slowly, she loosened her fingers, doing her best to smooth the cloth over his shoulders. Except that linen didn't smooth. Once wrinkled, it stayed wrinkled.

A bit like her life…

'Sorry,' she mouthed silently, only to discover that Zahir was still holding her.

Zahir was holding this girl he'd only just met, who was nothing like any girl he'd ever dated, had ever dreamed of dating, and for some reason he just couldn't let go.

He just wanted to keep her this close, with her hands on his shoulders, his hands at her waist keeping her close. To sail away with her into the sunset…

Well, that was the fantasy that this yacht had been built for.

'You can let go now,' she said. 'I won't fall over.'

'Really? Are you absolutely certain that you've got your sea-legs? Suppose there's another big wave?'

'Good point,' she said, making a point of looking at her watch. 'We'd better turn around and go back if I'm going to get you to London by six.'

He didn't want to go anywhere. He wanted to stay here with Diana and, as she pulled away, he said, 'Forget London. Tell me about the yacht.'

Diana swallowed.

What she really thought was that a yacht costing millions was a very clear demonstration of just how far out of her depth her heart had swum. Heading out to sea, but on its own and sinking fast.

'Does it matter what I think?'

'Would you want to spend your honeymoon on board her?' he pressed.

'She's lovely,' she said, putting on a big smile hoping that he wouldn't notice that she'd avoided the question. Putting a safe distance between them as, trailing her fingers along the handrail, she walked along the deck. Away from him. Then, because she couldn't help it, glancing back. He was standing just where she'd left him, his arm still extended, as if to keep her close. 'Does she have a name?' she asked. Anything to stop herself from going back.

'Yes…' He shook his head as if trying to think. 'Yes. I'm calling her *Star Gatherer*.'

Star...

'You just made that up!' she declared without thinking and, as if she'd somehow released him, he joined her at the rail, leaning over it, looking down into the water.

'I can see why, after last night, you might think so,' he said.

'No...'

Too late to deny it. 'Yes, Diana. But in fact the name comes from the poem, Arab Love-Song.' And he turned and leaned back against the rail, with the smile of a man who had just had everything he knew confirmed.

'The Maiden of the Morn will soon/Through Heaven stray and sing,/Star gathering.'

'Oh. That's beautiful.' Then, staring down into the water rushing past the side of the yacht, anywhere, rather than at him, 'How will you get her home?' she asked, seeking a subject less...incendiary. 'To Ramal Hamrah? Will you take her there yourself?'

'I wish I had that kind of time to spare. Unfortunately, at the moment the sky has first call on my time.' Better. Safer, she thought, raising an eyebrow. 'You might recall that I have an airline to get off the ground.'

'A yacht, an airline? Tell me, Zahir, do you have a bit of a thing about transport?'

'I'm in the travel business.'

'Oh, right. Well, I suppose that would explain it.'

'Jeff's mustering a permanent crew for the yacht and they'll bring her home. It'll give them a chance to put her through her paces, get to know her quirks, on the way.' Then, 'If I offered you a trip to Ramal Hamrah in her would you be as quick to turn me down a second time?'

'That depends. Would I have to share her with a bunch of freeloading journalists?' Before he could answer, she said, 'No, I'm kidding. I don't have that kind of time either.'

But this time as she turned her wrist to check the time, he took her hand, stopping her. 'We could always take her for a run across the Channel,' he said.

'The Channel? To *France*?' she squeaked.

His thumb was stroking the back of her fingers. 'We could have dinner in some little French café. I could take the train to Paris in the morning, while you return with the yacht.'

And the bit in between dinner and breakfast?

She couldn't breathe. It shouldn't be this hard to say no. If she just concentrated on that one word— morning. Remember that when morning came he'd be taking the fast train to Paris while her world would be in pieces.

Again.

And, on top of that, she wouldn't have a job.

'W-what about your dinner at the Mansion

House?' she stammered. 'If I don't get you back to London by six, James Pierce will call Sadie Redford and get me fired. He really doesn't like me.'

'I like you, that's all that matters.'

'Zahir…'

He lifted her hand to his lips, kissed the tips of her fingers. So sure of her…

'No…'

Maybe it was the first time a woman had ever said 'no' to him, or maybe it was the undisguised anguish in her voice, but she now had his full attention.

'I'm sorry,' she said, 'but my evening is already spoken for.'

'Your only task this evening is to drive me to the Mansion House.'

She shook her head. 'Sadie has arranged for someone else to stand in for me.'

'I don't want someone else!' She shook her head. 'Are you telling me, Metcalfe, that you have a date?'

And that, Diana realised, was the answer. If he thought she was involved with someone, he'd stop this…whatever *this* was. Save her from herself. Because, heaven help her, hard as she was trying, she was finding it impossible…

'Is that so unbelievable?' she asked. 'A minute ago you were inviting me to dinner in France.'

'I don't believe you.' Then, eyes narrowed, 'Tell me his name.'

'Freddy,' she said. How could she have been so lost in desire that the whole world had suddenly been filled with Zahir? Forgotten the child who was the centre of her world, who, she'd protected from the consequences of her own stupidity since the moment he had been conceived? 'His name is Freddy.'

Zahir felt his gut contract.

For a moment he hadn't believed her, had thought that she was clutching at the face-saving excuse he'd offered, protecting him as much as herself from the fallout of such an ill-considered venture. But one look at her face warned him that he was fooling himself.

She might have responded to his reckless kiss with all the passion at her command. She had certainly displayed all the signs of a woman betrayed when she'd thought he was involved with Lucy, but, whoever this Freddy was, he brought a whole new look to her face. A sweetness. A tenderness. Something that he'd fooled himself he'd seen when she'd looked up at him only moments before. When he'd had to force himself to say something stupid like 'all right?' to stop himself from picking her up and carrying her below, not as a choreographed move— the opening sequence in a slow dance that would lead inevitably to that inviting bed in the state-room—but as the beginning of something rare, un-expected, precious.

His suggestion that they take 'French leave' had

not, despite all appearances to the contrary, been driven by a libido racketing out of control, but because he wanted her with him. Couldn't bear the thought of watching her drive away…

For a moment he didn't move, but watched as she stood, one hand on the rail, her head slightly bowed, the sun lighting her hair like a rich halo around her face.

An illusion, he thought, turning abruptly and returning to the bridge.

'Time is short, Alan,' he snapped. 'I've seen enough. Let's get back to the yard so that I can sign the registration papers.'

CHAPTER EIGHT

SHEIKH ZAHIR did not invite Diana to join him while he signed the papers for his new yacht.

As she followed him ashore, he did not even look back as he dismissed her with an abrupt, 'I'll see you at the car, Diana. Be ready to leave in fifteen minutes.'

'Yes, sir,' she said, resisting the desire to say his name, feel it on her lips, reminding herself that was the way it was supposed to be.

Forget romance. The Cinderella fantasy was just that. A fantasy. She didn't believe in fairy tales and this wasn't the moment to lose her head. It was her job that mattered. This chance to move up the ladder. Get on. Get *somewhere*.

What she'd done back there had been right. For both of them. It hurt, but it would hurt far more afterwards when Zahir had returned to his real life and she was left with the pain.

The taxi was, probably always would be, just another fantasy, but becoming one of Capitol's senior drivers was within her grasp. Or it had been, until Sheikh Zahir had smiled at her and every bit of common sense had flown out of the window.

Before he'd kissed her. Before he'd danced with her, waltzing off with her heart…

Well, good luck to him. He could keep it as a souvenir of his trip to London. It wasn't as if she had any use for it.

What she needed was for the sheikh/chauffeur balance to be restored.

And it was.

Everything was back in balance.

So why did she feel so…bereft? So hollow? As if she'd just been offered the earth, the moon, the stars and had been too stupid, too scared to reach out and take them.

Because she hadn't been offered any of that.

What she'd been offered was an exotic, thrilling, world-well-lost one-night stand that she would never forget. But it would still just have been a one-night stand and without warning, tears filled her eyes, a lump rose in her throat and for a moment she couldn't move, but was bent double as the reality, the loss hit her.

She could never do that.

Never seize a moment. Take a chance. Grab at what life offered.

You made your mistakes and you lived with them.

* * *

'Your young lady doesn't look too hot, Zahir. If an hour sailing when the weather is this calm has that effect on her, it doesn't bode well for…'

Zahir stopped Alan with a look, then, unable to help himself, he turned to follow his gaze. Diana, arms around her waist and bent double, hadn't moved from the jetty, where he'd dismissed her, or walked away.

He muttered an oath beneath his breath but, before he could take more than a step, she straightened, swiping the palm of her hand over her cheek as she lifted her head in a gesture that echoed his own pull-yourself-together-and-get-over-it attempts to block out the pain as they'd sailed back to the boatyard.

Maybe her conscience was pricking her, he thought.

Last night, when he'd kissed her, danced with her, she hadn't been giving her 'Freddy' a second thought and today she'd been a heartbeat from giving him everything.

But for a freak wave she would have.

And what did that make him?

Maybe he should be giving his own conscience a wake-up call, it occurred to him, because last night, when she'd returned his kiss, had sung to him as she'd melted into his arms, he hadn't been giving his own future as much as a first thought. He'd been too busy making a fool of himself over a girl he'd only just met to spare a second or even a third thought for the young women being lined up for him to pick out a suitable wife.

Whatever Diana had been doing, his actions had been far worse…

'Whatever it was, she's over it now,' Alan said, watching her walk swiftly down the jetty until she rounded the building and was out of sight.

'So it would seem.' Uncapping his pen, he began to sign a stack of documents. He would do well to follow her example.

Enough. Diana slumped behind the wheel, staring at the car phone. At eighteen years old, mired in a world of guilt as her mother had threatened, her father had looked at her as if he didn't know her, she'd sworn *never again.*

She'd got lazy. Complacent.

It was easy to hold off the attentions of boys, men, when there was no attraction, no temptation, desire. Pete O'Hanlon had seen her looking at him as if he were something in a sweetshop window and he'd used that. But she wasn't blaming him. She'd wanted him, had seized the moment without a thought for the morrow and she had to live with that.

Her solace, her joy, was Freddy and she'd been content. But it had taken just one look from Zahir's slate-grey eyes, one smile, to let her know what she was missing. Melt the ice-wall she'd built around her heart.

She caught her breath, shaking her head as if to clear away all that romantic nonsense.

Not her heart. Nothing that noble.

What Sheikh Zahir al-Khatib had done with a single look was jump-start a hunger, a need that was so far beyond her experience that she hadn't recognised the danger until it was too late.

Until she was experiencing feelings that were so strong that for a moment she had been in danger of repeating history…

No. This had to stop now. Now, before she wavered and did something really stupid and told him that Freddy was five years old. That her date was a classroom visit. Because, if she told him that, he'd know…

She reached out to hit the fast dial on the car phone to call Sadie, ask her to take her off this job— what excuse she'd make she didn't know, but she'd think of something. The phone rang before her finger made contact, making her jump nearly out of her skin, the caller ID warning her that Sadie had got in first. She was no doubt calling to update her on who would be driving Sheikh Zahir this evening so that she could pass on the good news.

She jabbed 'receive', but, before she could speak, Sadie said, 'Diana! At last! I've been calling you for the best part of an hour on this phone and your cellphone.'

'Have you?' She frowned, rubbing her hands over her pockets. No cellphone. 'I must have left it in my jacket…'

'I don't care where you left it! Where, in heaven's name, have you *been*?'

'Well…'

'No, don't bother to answer that. I can guess,' she said cuttingly.

What?

Diana straightened. 'Look, I'm sorry, but Sheikh Zahir…'

'Please! I don't want to know. I just want you to listen to me. You are not to come back to the yard. You will be met at the car park outside The King's Head in Little Markham by Michael Jenkins. He'll drive the Mercedes back from there. Sheikh Zahir's personal assistant has arranged for another car to be on hand to take him back to the hotel. You…'

'Whoa! Back up, Sadie. What on earth has happened?'

'You have to ask?'

Confused, miserable, she wasn't in the mood for games. 'Apparently I do,' she snapped back with uncharacteristic sharpness.

'You'd like me to read you the diary column from the midday edition of *The Courier*?'

'What?'

'Maybe it will jog your memory if I tell you that the headline is "The Sheikh and the Chauffeur"? Or do you want all the gory details of how Sheikh Zahir al-Khatib was seen gazing into the eyes of his pretty chauffeur as he waltzed her around Berkeley Square at midnight?'

'How on earth—?'

'For heaven's sake, everyone with a camera phone is an amateur paparazzo these days, Di! Even if the snapper didn't recognise Sheikh Zahir, a man dancing with his chauffeur made it a story. The fact that he looks lost to the world makes it the kind of story that *The Courier* was always going to run in its diary column. I don't imagine it took them more than two minutes to identify Sheikh Zahir. He's not exactly a stranger to the gossip pages.'

'He isn't?'

'He's a billionaire bachelor, Diana, what do you think?'

Think?

Who was thinking?

'Oh—'

'Don't say it!'

'I wasn't going to.' She swallowed. 'I was going to say that it's not the way it must look.'

Not *exactly*.

'I'm afraid the way it looks is all people are interested in.'

'No-o-o-o…'

Sadie just sighed.

'No. For what it's worth, I believe you, but it makes no difference. It's a good story and that's all the tabloids care about. What *does* matter is that we're under siege here.'

'Siege?'

'The hunters are out and you are the prey. Your name wasn't in the paper but it didn't take the sleaze-merchants long to find out which company is chauffeuring the Sheikh around London this week. I think we can safely assume that by now they have got not only your name but probably know the colour of the polish on your toenails.'

'I'm not wearing polish on…' She stopped. Sadie was speaking metaphorically. 'Sadie, I am *so* sorry. I promise you it was all perfectly…'

Innocent. She'd been going to say innocent. It wasn't true.

Innocent didn't feel the way she'd felt last night when he'd kissed her. When he'd held her. Had raised her hand to his lips. She remembered the way her skin had warmed to his touch. How her lips had wanted more of him. The sweet liquid meltdown in the pit of her belly as he'd waltzed her around the Square. Made her feel like a princess.

As for today…

She had compared her foolishness to her moment of madness with Pete O'Hanlon. He had never looked at her the way Zahir had looked at her. Had never made her feel the way that Zahir…

'Diana!'

She jumped as Sadie shouted her name. Realised that she had been talking to her, expected some kind of response.

'I'm sorry. I'm in shock.'

'Get a grip. You've got to keep your head. No doubt it'll just be a nine-minute wonder—'

'Less,' she said, determined to reassure Sadie.

It was already over.

'Let's hope so. I want you to take the rest of the week off. You've already got next week booked as leave for Freddy's half term holiday and Sheikh Zahir will have left the country by then. And yes, before you ask, you'll get paid. Your time will go on Sheikh Zahir's account as a disruption expense. I hope he thinks one dance was worth it.'

'No…' That wasn't fair. 'Sadie…'

But she was listening to the dialling tone. For a moment she sat there, numb with shock, then picked up her jacket and found her cellphone. She kept it switched off while she was driving, but the minute she thumbed it on she saw that she had more than a dozen voicemail messages.

Several from Sadie. A terse 'Call me' from her mother. A couple from her father, who'd been getting calls from neighbours, newspapers. Three from tabloid journalists offering her money for her story—how on earth had they got this number?

There were even two calls from gossip magazines offering sky's-the-limit deals for her 'Cinderella' story, with pictures of her and her family in their ordinary little terraced house in Putney.

They knew where she lived?

And finally one from an infamous Public Relations guru warning her to say nothing, sign nothing, until she'd talked to him.

It was like a verbal car wreck. Horrible, but so compelling that she couldn't hit the 'disconnect' switch, and Sadie's warning finally sank in.

These people wouldn't quit until they'd dredged up everything. How long would it be before someone was telling them that no one knew who Freddy's father was? Implying that she didn't know. That would really give them something to get their teeth into…

'If you've finished calling your boyfriend?' Zahir said, opening the rear door of the car. He'd removed his jacket and, as he tossed it into the back of the car the phone in her hand began to ring.

Startled, she gave a little shriek and dropped it at her feet, where it continued to ring.

'It's not…' she began, but her voice was shaking. Everything was shaking. 'I wasn't…' The voicemail cut in and the phone finally stopped ringing.

'Diana?' Zahir's soft query, no longer angry, just velvet concern, only made things worse. He opened the driver's door, folded himself up so that he was on her level. 'What on earth is the matter?' Unable to speak, she just hung on to the steering wheel, her forehead against her hands. 'Please… How can I help if you do not tell me?'

She shook her head, her throat choked with rage and misery. At her feet, the phone began to ring again.

Zahir reached in, picked it up and answered the call with an abrupt, 'Yes?' then listened for a moment before disconnecting the call without speaking again. Then he turned it off and placed it in his pocket.

'Who was it?'

'Someone from a magazine called *Hot Gossip*. The woman addressed me by name?' It was a question, one that required an answer, but all she could manage was a groan.

How useless was that? How pitiful? As if sitting here drowning in the unfairness of it all was going to help.

He had to know.

She had to tell him.

And, making an effort, she sat back, scrubbed at her cheeks with her hands and said, 'The office have been trying to get in touch with me ever since our nightingale two-step became public knowledge at midday.' She turned to face him, wanting to be sure that he understood. 'That was when *The Courier* hit the streets.' When he didn't immediately respond, 'I imagine Mr Pierce has been calling you too.'

'Yes,' he said, 'I imagine he has. But he can wait. I'm more concerned about you. What do you want me to do?'

'You?' She shook her head. 'There's nothing either of us can do except get on with life. It's all we can ever do. Get on with it. And to do that I have to get home.' Then, seeing his doubtful expression, 'Don't worry, it's all been sorted.' She began to explain the arrangements that Sadie and James had made but he brushed them aside.

'You can't go home, Diana. The paparazzi will have already staked out your house. It will be bedlam.'

She'd seen such things on the television news. Politicians caught with their pants down, being door-stepped by the media. It wouldn't be like that. This wasn't the kind of story that made the nine o'clock news, but she had no doubt it would be uncomfortable and her father was there on his own.

She glanced at her watch, checking the time. No,

not on his own. He'd have been forced to confront them to fetch Freddy from school…

She groaned. 'Please, Zahir, get in. I have to get home right now!'

He didn't move. 'I'm so sorry, Diana.'

'Don't…' She shook her head. 'This is my fault. You were just happy. If I'd behaved like a professional…'

'Don't be selfish with the guilt, *ya habibati*,' he said, taking her hands, easing her to her feet, forcing her to look at him. 'There's always enough of that to go around.' Then, 'Call your family. Tell them that James will come and pick up your passport, an overnight bag. I can't stop this, but I can get you away until it's blown over…'

'What?'

What had he called her? A fool, an idiot, no doubt. Well, he had every right and he hadn't done it unkindly, but almost tenderly. She shook her head. As if it mattered…

'You expect me to run away and leave my family, the people I love, to face this on their own?'

'If you're not there…'

'What? The journalists will just go away? They won't ring endlessly, harass my parents? The neighbours? Freddy…'

The horror of it hit her full force and, as her knees sagged, he released one hand to catch her, hold her close. And for a moment she leaned against him, clinging to him for support, for his strength, as the awfulness of it swept over her.

It wouldn't just be at the yard. It would be at her home, at school.

And how long would it be before someone was gossiping about Freddy? Saw the possibilities of making a little hard cash out of old photographs, speculating on just who his father might be?

She didn't care about herself. She had protected Freddy then. Had outfaced her mother's threats, her father's tears, had even told the Child Support Agency where they could stick their money. It would take more than a bunch of journalists to shake it out of her. But it would make her visible, make Freddy visible. Drag it all up again, the gossip. And he was getting older, his face was firming up; if people started to look again, what might they see?

No.

Who would ever believe that Pete O'Hanlon would have even looked at the last virgin in the sixth form? But it would still be a total nightmare for her parents.

Terrifying for a little boy.

Zahir was right. Her home, the place where she could hold out against the world, knowing that her parents would support her, whatever she did, whatever it cost them, was no longer a haven.

As she straightened, stood on her own two feet, she shivered. 'It doesn't matter about me, Zahir, but I can't leave my family to deal with this on their own. I have to get my parents and Freddy out of there too.'

Freddy.

There it was. Zahir had known. He'd heard this man's name on her lips, and seen her face as she'd spoken of him, but even while his head had understood what she was telling him, his heart had refused to believe it. Had clung to some forlorn hope…

It was his heart that had called her his beloved.

That she could never return his feelings, that he would never be her *habibi*, made no difference. She had made the nightingale sing for him, her smile had made the stars shine beneath his feet. She had given him a moment that he would carry with him always, but in doing so had brought this horror crashing about her. The least he could do in return was offer his protection to her and to all those she loved.

Even now, as she looked up at him, as he felt the flutter of her pulse against his palm, he could scarcely believe that she loved another man. Her eyes seemed to tell him that all she wanted was for him to hold her against his heart, enfold her in his arms. Keep her from harm.

'It is done,' he said. 'Call them and tell them to be ready.'

She had mockingly called him 'Galahad' and she was right to mock. Even now, when there were a dozen things he had to do to make this happen, he wanted nothing more than to hold her, promise her his world.

'Zahir…' His name on her lips was so sweet, but he did not look at her as he stepped back.

Did not dare look. What he was feeling meant nothing. He wasn't Galahad offering her a pure heart. There was no fairy tale, no romance here.

Worse, no honour.

All he'd had to offer Diana Metcalfe was one night in his bed and, in making that offer, he'd broken the cardinal rules on which he'd so prided himself. Never to become involved with anyone who might get hurt. There wasn't a thing he could do to prevent that now, other than give her sanctuary.

'Call your family while I talk to James and make the necessary arrangements so that we can leave before someone uses your cellphone to track us here.'

'Where are we going?'

Not we. Never we. He could not go with her…

'You and your family…' he could not bring himself to say her lover's name '…will be my guests at Nadira Creek for as long as you need a refuge. And I promise you that, while you are there, it will be off limits to journalists.'

Off limits to him.

Zahir retrieved his jacket from the rear of the car,

dug out his own phone and, leaving Diana to call home, he rang James Pierce.

'Just listen,' he said, cutting him off before he could start. 'I want a private jet ready to leave Farnborough airfield early this evening.' He checked his watch. 'No later than seven o'clock. As soon as that's arranged, call Sadie Redford and tell her to send someone she trusts with her life to pick up a party of three and their luggage from Diana's home…'

He opened the car door.

'…I'm sorry, Freddy. Please, sweetie…' Diana paused with the endearment on her lips, looked up. Her eyes were full of tears but there was nothing he could do. No comfort he could offer her. No comfort for him…

'I need your address,' he said. She blinked, not quite with him. Never with him… 'For James.'

'Oh, right.' Then, 'Actually, it might be better if they leave the house by the back way through Aunt Alice's. Her garden backs on to ours. Ninety-two, Prince Albert Street.'

'Aunt Alice's,' he repeated. 'Will she be coming too?'

She almost smiled but the dimple didn't quite make it. 'No, Zahir. She's not a real aunt, just my mother's best friend.'

He nodded, walking away from the car as he gave James the details. 'Tell Sadie Redford the change in plans. Tell her… Tell her I'll bring the Mercedes back to London when I've dropped Diana at the airport. She can have someone pick it up at the hotel.'

'You're not going with her, then?'

There was something in James's tone that put an edge in his voice. He ignored it. 'Why would I do that when I'm a guest at the Mansion House tonight? Something you might mention to any journalist you encounter who expresses an interest in my immediate plans. But you'll have to cancel the Paris trip. I'm bringing forward the announcement of Ramal Hamrah Airways to tomorrow morning and I'll be going home straight after that.'

Ameerah would not forgive him for missing her party, but neither would Hanif and Lucy appreciate a Pied Piper trail of journalists invading their children's party.

At least he would make his mother happy. Hopefully give his father the grandson he desired. He owed them that.

CHAPTER NINE

IT WAS a nightmare.

Zahir insisted on driving—and he was right, she was in no fit state to handle the big car—pushing the speed limit all the way to Farnborough. He'd been kind, gentle with her, but it didn't take a genius to see that he couldn't wait to rid himself of her.

Who could blame him?

The moment they arrived at the airfield—one favoured by the kind of men for whom the private jet was the standard form of transport and ironically a regular run for the limo drivers—he made his excuses.

'I have to go,' he said as, with one of the VIP hostesses standing by to whisk her away, he made a formal little bow. 'Your family will be with you very shortly.'

'You'd better get a move on,' she said, forcing herself to look at her watch, to look away from his beautiful face, even though she knew it would be the last time she'd see him. Doing her best to keep it light.

'It won't do to keep the Prime Minister waiting.' For heaven's sake, she barely knew the man. Why then, did it feel like the end of the world? 'But try not to get a speeding ticket or that'll be another black mark against my name.'

'I'll take care, but if I miss the dinner the press will leap to the conclusion that we are...' He faltered, a gesture filling the gap.

He was protecting her? Or was he protecting himself?

It didn't matter!

'You don't have to draw a picture, Zahir. Go. Now. I'll be fine.'

And with another bow he turned and walked away from her. It was odd. He was wearing a casual suit, and yet in her mind he was wearing robes...

'Would you like to freshen up while you're waiting, Miss Metcalfe?' The hostess, who had been standing at a discreet distance while Zahir had been with her, tactfully eased her into the sanctuary of a luxurious washroom where she offered a box of tissues.

'I'll come and fetch you when the rest of your party arrive.'

It was only then that she realised that tears were pouring down her face, dripping on to her shirt, soaking it.

Try as she might to forget, all she could think about was Zahir dismissing the dinner as unimportant when he was suggesting they sail across to France in his yacht. But for a freak wave they might even now be putting into some quaint Normandy harbour where she'd be waking in his arms to a French dawn, unaware of the furore...

She shook her head. It would, in the end, only have made things worse. She'd done the right thing. Even if it meant that Zahir thought she was...

Well, he must have a pretty low opinion of a woman who'd responded so fervently to the kisses of someone who was practically a stranger when she was involved with another man.

Had wanted him to do more than kiss her.

No wonder he'd dropped her and run.

She made an effort to stem the flow of tears she had no business shedding. Tidied herself up, directed the hand-drier at her shirt—as shirt days went, this was having a bad one—to dry herself off.

Putting on a front before her mother arrived.

Some hope.

She must have broken some kind of record with her packing, because Diana was still struggling to put on lipstick with a shaky hand when the hostess came for her.

Sadie's father, Daniel Redford, the man who owned Capitol Cars but now left the day-to-day business to his daughter, had brought her family to the airfield in the back of the old black London cab that he used as a town car. Clever of Sadie. Far less noticeable than one of the burgundy Capitol cars. And kind too, to call on her father to help out an employee who'd given her such a headache.

'I'm so grateful, Mr Redford…' Oh, damn, the tears were threatening again.

'It was no trouble. I enjoyed the cloak-and-dagger. We got away clean as a whistle,' he said. Such a sweet man. 'And don't worry about the yard,' he added, a reassuring hand to her elbow. The hacks are getting short shrift there. It'll be nothing but a nine-minute wonder, you'll see.'

Her mother, who'd apparently rushed home from work when the phone calls had started, was not sweet.

On the contrary, she was livid, and it was only Freddy's presence that kept her from speaking her mind. Her father, painfully, seemed unable to look at her. Even Freddy—normally the sweetest-natured of boys—had turned sulky because she'd missed the parents' evening at school.

So much for putting him first…

Maybe it was a good thing that Zahir hadn't stayed to witness the fact that not one member of her family was talking to her. The 'not again…' looks her mother was giving her. At least until they were ushered aboard the private jet, at which point she was too distracted by the kind of luxury that only the super-rich could afford to keep it up.

It was dark, the middle of the night, when they arrived at Nadira Creek. Even so, the air was soft, warm, scented with exotic blooms, and, as she looked up, the stars were like diamonds scattered over black velvet.

Zahir was right. It was awesome.

Like the villa that had been put at their disposal. What she'd seen of it was like something out of a dream. Not that she'd seen much. They were all too shattered by the swift turn of events, the rush, the tension.

But finally Freddy was tucked up and at last she was able to get out of her working clothes and take a shower in a bathroom that was about the size of her bedroom back home, using the kind of soaps that she'd only ever heard of.

Afterwards, wrapped in the softest towelling robe, she checked on her parents. They were already asleep, but, when she tried to follow suit, her mind wouldn't let go. All she could think about was Zahir. What he was doing. What he was thinking.

Had he been mobbed on arrival at the Mansion House? Probably not. With heads of state and cabinet ministers attending, security would be tight.

At the hotel?

Almost certainly. Not that he would say anything. He'd just have given the waiting photographers one of his show-stopping smiles. The kind that meant nothing.

But what was he feeling?

Anger. With himself, no doubt, for behaving like a fool. But with her too, for what he must feel had been her deceit.

She might not have lied about Freddy and if he'd asked her outright she would have told him the truth. But what she hadn't said had left him with a contradiction and he would not, could not, think well of her.

When the pale silver edge of dawn filtered through the lattice shutters of the balcony it came as a relief. She pushed one back and caught her first glimpse of Nadira Creek, shimmering, a pale and milky pink in the early morning light.

Shreds of mist clung to cliffs that rose on the far side of the water. Draped itself like silk chiffon amongst the date palms and what, unbelievably, looked like pomegranate trees in the gardens that sloped away from the terrace below her.

If yesterday had ended on a nightmare, today was beginning with something like a dream.

She quickly showered, dressed and, after looking in on Freddy, still dead to the world, she went downstairs to a huge sitting room where sofas, cushions and beautiful rugs were strewn across the dark polished floor.

But she didn't linger there.

Wide French windows stood open to an arcaded courtyard and she walked out into the misty dawn, drawn by the sound of water trickling down a narrow rill to steps that led down to a lily-covered pool. Beside it, a raised open-sided pavilion was almost hidden beneath a vast fig tree.

Like the house, it was furnished with luxuriously rich carpets and silk cushions, inviting her to curl up and sleep until the world forgot her. Before she gave in to the temptation, a phone resting on a low carved table, the only thing that was out of place in this Arabian Nights fantasy, burbled softly.

She looked around, but there was no one else in sight and, when it rang again, she picked it up. 'Hello?'

For a moment no one answered and, absolutely certain that she'd done the wrong thing, she was about to hang up when Zahir's voice said, 'Diana...'

Just her name, like a sigh, and her legs seemed to buckle beneath her so that somehow she was lying amongst the cushions, for all the world like some pampered houri waiting for her lord.

'Zahir...'

'It's early,' he said. 'You could not sleep?'

'The sun is telling me that it's early, but my body clock is telling me I should be at work,' she replied.

'So you're exploring?'

'Nothing so energetic. Just enjoying the view.

It's beautiful, Zahir. Totally wasted on a bunch of journalists…'

She stopped. Not the wisest thing to have said, but when had she ever thought before she spoke?

'They have their uses,' he replied, with what sounded like a smile colouring his voice. 'But rest assured, no journalist will ever enjoy the view from where you are lying now.'

'Oh.'

Diana swallowed, blushing. What was it about the word 'lying' that was so…suggestive? And how did he know…?

She almost felt as if he could see her, touch her. As if he were there with her amongst the silken pillows, his hand cradling her hip, his mouth…

She cleared her throat. Struggled, determinedly, despite the unwillingness of the cushions to let her go, into a sitting position. Then, feeling slightly more in control, said, 'Do you want me to go and find someone for you? I haven't seen anyone, but the doors were open so I imagine someone is about.'

'No need. I just wanted to be sure that you'd arrived safely. That you're comfortable.'

'Comfortable is rather understating the case. I know your resort is supposed to be luxurious, but this is something else. Not at all what I'd expected.'

'Oh?' He sounded amused. 'What did you expect?'

'I don't know,' she said, looking up at the beautiful house built into the rock. The cool blue tiles of the arcaded courtyard, the wide wooden balcony with its fretwork shutters. Another floor above that. 'I somehow imagined a series of cottages set in a garden.'

Definitely not this Arabian Nights palace that looked as if it had been there for all time.

'Maybe I've seen too many travel programmes on the television.'

'Rest assured, Diana. Your imagination is in full working order. The resort is on the other side of the creek. There is still work going on there, little privacy. I thought you'd be more comfortable in the house. Hamid, my steward, will take you across the creek in the boat, give you the tour whenever you wish. Does your father enjoy fishing?'

'I don't think he's ever tried,' she said. 'But he loves boats.'

'Which explains the book of nautical knots.'

'Oh, no, that was for…' Her hand flew to her mouth, stopping herself from saying the name. *Idiot!*

'I see.'

Did he? Had Freddy been mentioned in the newspapers? *'Single mother chauffeur dances with sheikh in the street…'* would appeal to a certain section of the press.

The silence stretched to breaking point until she could no longer bear it.

'Zahir…'

'Diana…'

They spoke at the same time, apparently both equally anxious to fill the void.

'What is it, Diana? Tell me…'

Tell him what?

That she wished he were here with her? That she'd wept when he'd left her? That there would always be an emptiness in her heart without him?

For heaven's sake, she'd only met him days ago.

But then, how long did it take to fall in love? She had no yardstick against which to judge her feelings. And even if it was love, so what?

He didn't believe in it. He'd told her…

'It was nothing,' she said. Nothing that she had any right to say. Nothing that made any sense. 'How was your Mansion House dinner?'

'Do you want a blow-by-blow account of what I ate? Or a précis of the Prime Minister's state of the nation speech?' he asked. When she didn't answer, he said, 'No, I thought not.'

She glanced at her watch, calculated the time difference. 'Actually, shouldn't you be on your way to Paris?'

'Paris will have to wait. I've brought my schedule forward to take advantage of the unexpectedly high interest in my affairs. I'm announcing the new airline today.'

'Oh, well, good luck.'

'I think I can guarantee that every seat at the press conference will be taken.' Then, before she could think of a response, 'I have to go. Just ask Hamid for whatever you want, Diana. Do not be shy.'

About to say, Shy? You've got me confused with some other Diana... But, before she could speak, she was listening to the dialling tone.

'Mu-um!'

Freddy came slowly down the steps, rubbing his eyes, trailing his teddy behind him so that he bumped on every one. A sure sign that he needed a hug.

She replaced the receiver and swept him up in her arms and he clung to her, not too big, too grown-up for a cuddle today. She knew how he felt. She could do with one herself.

He recovered first.

But then her condition was terminal...

'Is that the sea?' he asked, perking up as he looked over her shoulder.

'It certainly is,' she said, gathering herself, making an effort at brightness.

'Is there a beach?' Now he wriggled, eager to get down and explore. 'Can we make a sandcastle? Does Grandpa know?' He hit the ground running, teddy abandoned at her feet. 'Grandpa! Grandpa!'

She picked it up, followed him, was just in time to see him skid to a halt at the sight of Hamid, the white-robed steward who'd shown them to their rooms when they'd arrived.

'Good morning, *sitti*,' he said with a low bow. 'I hope you are comfortable?'

'We're very comfortable thank you, Hamid.'

'Sheikh Zahir wished me to assure you that his house is at your disposal. You are to make yourself completely at home. It is his wish that you enjoy your stay as his guest.'

His house? This was where Zahir lived? As in his actual home?

No wonder he'd sounded amused at her assumption that this was part of the holiday resort.

And he'd already spoken to Hamid. Had his servant put him through to the summer house? Well, of course he had. Why else would the phone have rung there?

Her hand went to her chest to calm the sudden wild beating.

It meant nothing. Nothing…

Hamid folded himself up so that he was on the same level as Freddy. 'What would the young sheikh like for his breakfast?'

Freddy shrank behind her skirt.

'His name is Freddy and the shyness won't last,' she assured the man. 'He usually has cereals. Maybe some juice?' She made it a question, unsure what was on offer.

He smiled at the boy. 'Maybe you would like to

try a fig? Some yoghurt with honey? Or what about pancakes?'

'Pancakes?'

'I was with Sheikh Zahir in America. They eat pancakes for breakfast there, did you know?'

Freddy, eyes wide, shook his head.

He certainly knew how to win the heart of a small boy.

'And the *sitti*?' he said, rising. 'Pomegranate juice? New bread. Goats' cheese.'

Sitti? That was her?

'Why don't you surprise us, Hamid?' she said. 'Maybe tea?'

'Darjeeling? Earl Grey?'

'Darjeeling. Thank you,' she said, letting out a silent 'whew' as Hamid bowed and left them. *Goats' cheese for breakfast*? How the other half lived.

Then, laughing—something that after yesterday afternoon she'd thought she'd never do again—she said, 'Okay, young sheikh, I think we need to get you washed and dressed before breakfast.'

Zahir tossed the cellphone on the desk and dragged a hand over his unshaven face. It was six in the morning at Nadira, the best time of day, when the sun would be low, turning the rocks and sand pink. The creek deserted but for a few night fishermen returning with their catch.

And today Diana was walking in his garden, stepping where he'd walked, touching things that were precious to him. Lying where he had lain against the silk cushions in his summer house, surrounded by the scent of jasmine. But not with him. He could not go there while she was there. Could never see her again. Must never call her again.

He picked up the little book that lay on the desk in front of him. The book that Diana had thrust into his hand just before he'd fled the airfield, asking him to give it to Ameerah, and for a moment he held it against his lips, as if to transfer her touch to him.

He'd hated leaving her on her own, even though it would only have been for a little while. He'd wished to meet her parents, apologise as a man should, for having put them through such an ordeal. But to do that would have meant witnessing her face lighting up as this Freddy walked through the door. To offer his hand to a man who possessed what he most desired. And keep that desire from his own eyes.

He'd been a fool to ask Hamid to put him through to the summer house, would not have done so if he hadn't been assured that she was on her own.

What could he possibly say to her when all the words that burned in his heart were forbidden to him? When all they could talk about was a formal dinner he'd attended? His press conference…

'You've got forty minutes, Zahir.' James looked

at his untouched breakfast, the newspapers that lay unopened by his tray, and made no comment. He'd been pointedly not making any comment since he'd arrived back in London yesterday evening. 'I'll get you some fresh coffee.'

'Don't bother. Just see that this is gift-wrapped and delivered to Ameerah,' he said, handing James the book. 'It's from Diana,' he said, finding some consolation in being able to say her name. 'To go with the snow globe.'

'*The Princess and the Frog*?' James said, looking at the book, then at him. 'What on earth has that got to do with the Snow Queen?'

'The Snow Queen?'

Glacial, icily beautiful. He could see how the subject might appeal to a glass-blower but he was, he decided, glad that it had been broken. Its replacement might not have had any intrinsic value but it had warmth…

Or was that an illusion? Was it Diana, weaving her tale for him, who'd given the toy a touch of magic?

James was still awaiting an explanation and, with a shrug, he said, 'I'm afraid there was a slight accident at the airport. A small boy in a hurry. A concrete pavement. I had to find an instant replacement.' Then, 'Nothing nearly so precious.'

'You should have mentioned it. I'll get someone to sort out an insurance claim.'

'Let it go, James. Let it go. In fact, forget this too,' he said, dropping the book in the waste basket. 'We've more important things to do.'

It was late when he arrived in Ramal Hamrah, but Zahir had warned his mother to expect him. He wanted this over with and he'd changed on the plane, abandoning his suit and tie for traditional robes.

For a formal visit to his mother, *this* formal visit, only traditional robes would do. The gossamer-fine black and gold camel hair cloak. A *keffiyeh* held in place by a simple camel halter.

His mother was alone, standing in the centre of her drawing room—a princess granting an audience. He touched his forehead, his heart, bowed low.

'*Sitti*,' he said. My lady. Only then did he approach to kiss her.

She was slight and, as he straightened, he stood nearly a foot taller, but her slap as she struck his cheek with the flat of her hand had force enough to drive him back a step, ring his ears.

Futile, then, to hope that she hadn't seen the newspaper.

He bowed a second time, an acknowledgement that her anger was justified, her rebuke accepted without argument.

'I am here to inform you, *sitti,* that I am at your

command, ready to meet with, take a bride from the young women you have chosen,' he said.

'You think it is that simple?' she enquired, her voice dripping ice. 'Yesterday I met with the Attiyah family. They have no male heir and mothers are lining up to make an alliance for their sons with Shula, their oldest daughter. You, my son, for reasons that I cannot begin to fathom, seem to be favoured above all, but this morning I received a note from the girl's mother, asking me to deny a rumour that you have installed your mistress at your house at Nadira.'

Well, that explained the slap. Embarrassing his mother was the sin.

'I will assure Kasim al-Attiyah, as I assure you,' he replied, 'that Miss Metcalfe is not my mistress. I have simply given her and her family temporary refuge...'

'Her father is not the one you have to convince. He is a man and he knows that all men carry their brains between their legs.'

Having got that off her chest, her face softened and she laid the hand she'd struck him with against his cheek. 'Shula al-Attiyah is a modern woman, Zahir. She is well-educated, travelled, as are all the young women I've chosen for you to meet. I sought a true match for you, my son. Someone who understands your world. Who will be the kind of life partner you would choose for yourself.' She let her hand fall, turned away. 'But this is the twenty-first century and no Ramal Hamrah girl worth her salt is going to ally herself with a man who's photo-graphed dancing in a London street with his—'

'Mother,' he warned.

'With a woman who, even now, is living in your house with her child. A boy the gossips in the souk are saying is your son!'

'What did you say?'

Zahir heard his mother's words clearly enough but they made no sense. He reran them over and over…

Boy…

Son…

'Is it true?' she demanded, while he was still trying to come to terms with what she'd said.

He shook his head. It couldn't be true…

And yet, almost like a movie running in his brain, he saw again the carrier with the books she'd bought. Saw himself opening it. Children's books, she'd said. *Children's* books. Plural. The fairy tale book had been for Ameerah. But the other one, the book of knots, that was the kind of gift you'd buy for a small boy…

She'd lied to him. No…

His gesture, pushing the thought away, was emphatic.

She had not lied.

He, in an offhand remark, had provided her with

the excuse and she'd grabbed at it, using it to keep him at a distance. And it would have worked but for the photograph in *The Courier*—

'You do not seem certain, my son.'

He was dragged back to the present, to the reality of what was rather than the might-have-been, by a suggestion of anxiety in his mother's voice, sensing that beneath her aristocratic posture was a genuine fear that, even in this most basic duty—to make a marriage that would bring honour to his family—he was about to fail her.

'You may rest assured that I met Miss Metcalfe for the first time this week,' he said, and his heart tore at the unmistakable sag in her aristocratic posture as the tension left her.

It was recovered in a moment and, with a gracious nod, she dismissed him. 'Very well. Call on me tomorrow at five and I will introduce you to Shula al-Attiyah.'

CHAPTER TEN

ZAHIR'S first impulse on leaving his mother's house was to drive straight to Nadira to demand answers. But not dressed like this. Not wearing the robes in which he'd just made a commitment to marriage, an alliance that would bring honour to his family.

This was not the man who'd kissed, danced in the streets as if his life were his own.

By the time he'd showered, changed and was racing out across the desert, however, common sense began to assert itself.

It would be the early hours of the morning before he reached Nadira and he'd already caused Diana enough grief with his foolishness.

He slowed, pulled off the road and, wrapping himself in a heavy camel-hair cloak, began to walk.

He'd sworn he'd stay away from Diana, for once do his duty. It was his cousin, Hanif—a man for whom duty was as life itself—who had warned him that marriage was a lifelong commitment. Not something to be entered into lightly, but wholeheartedly.

And he was right. There must be no looking back over his shoulder. No lingering sense of unfinished business.

With the memory of Diana doubled up in silent agony on the quay seared into his mind, he had no doubt that there was unfinished business here.

Why had she lied to him?

He stopped. No. That was wrong. She had not lied. But neither had she contradicted him when he'd offered his own insulting interpretation. But what was he to think when one moment she was lost to the world in his arms, the next minute on edge, untouchable, desperate to get back to London?

He'd seen her pain, but had written it off as her own guilty conscience troubling her. Had turned away, so blinded by hurt, by a sense of betrayal, that he'd been unable to accept what, deep down, he'd known. That the betrayal was his.

His future was written. He could offer her nothing, whereas Diana...

Yesterday she could have made a fortune selling her 'story' to the press. She wouldn't even have had to sex things up. All she'd have had to do was tell it like it was and the entire world would have been enchanted.

As he was.

At first sight.

She hadn't even considered it. Not for a minute. From the moment she'd been told what had happened she'd thought only of her son. Her family. Of him. Apologising to him as if this was in some way her fault.

She had a son!

How old was he? Did he look like her? Or his absent father? That he was absent he did not doubt. She'd told him that she lived with her parents. Knew that she worked hard to provide for him…

He knew so little.

And yet so much. He knew that she was a loving mother. He's seen her face, tender as she'd spoken the boy's name. It was a look that had torn his heart out.

It was a look he'd seen tonight on his own mother's face as she'd lain her hand against his cheek.

Furious as she was, the unconditional love remained. All she cared about was his happiness, a fact she'd demonstrated in searching for a bride who would please him, rather than the daughter-in-law she must have hoped for—an educated, travelled career woman, rather than a stay-at-home girl whose only thought would be to provide her with grandchildren.

He walked until pre-dawn turned the sky grey, coming to terms with what he must do. His parting from Diana had been abrupt, painful. It had not been done well and, before he could move on, embrace the life that awaited him, he had to thank her for what she'd done. Show her that he honoured her.

Zahir let himself into the quiet house just as dawn was turning from pink to gold and, for a moment, he stood in the tranquil courtyard and let the peace of the place surround him.

He had an apartment in the city, but he'd made no secret of the fact that this house belonged to his heart. That it was his home. His future. The place where he would, eventually—when he had time— bring his bride, make a family.

It was hardly surprising the gossips were having a field day, he thought as he crossed to the steps that led down to the pavilion.

Someone had beaten him to it. Diana…?

He paused at the foot of the veranda steps, listening to the soft sigh of her breath. Had she slept amongst the cushions, as he did on warm nights?

One step would bring him to her side. Her hair, tumbled over the silk, would be his to touch. Her cheek, her lips…

The thought made the heat sing in his blood.

'No…' The word was wrenched from him but, as he turned away, a tousled head appeared from amongst the cushions. Eyes the colour of a spring hedgerow met his.

Blinked.

Like Diana's. The same colour. The same shape, but not Diana's eyes. This was her child? Her son...

How could he doubt it?

The boy's hair was darker, but the curl matched hers. And his dimpled smile, like hers, went straight to his heart, capturing it in an instant as he sat up, yawned and said, 'Hello.' Then, 'Who are you?'

Zahir touched his hand to his heart, bowed formally. 'My name is Zahir bin Ali bin Khatib al-Khatib.' Then, when the boy giggled, he lowered himself to the veranda steps so that he was the same level as the child and said, 'And you, *ya habibi*? What is your name?'

'I'm Freddy.' Then, as if realising that this came up short, he said, 'I'm Frederick Trueman Metcalfe. I was named after Fiery Fred, the finest bowler who ever played cricket for Yorkshire and England.' The words came out all in a rush, as if it was something he'd heard many times but did not quite understand. He suddenly looked less certain. 'At least that's what my grandpa says.'

'It's a fine name. And are you going to follow in Mr Trueman's footsteps and play cricket for England?'

'No. I'm going to be a footballer.'

Zahir managed to hide a smile. 'We must all follow our own star, Freddy. Dream our own dreams.'

Live our own lives?

No! No...

Then, concerned, 'Are you alone?'

'I was looking for Mummy. She wasn't in her room when I woke up so I came here. She was here yesterday.'

They had both come here looking for her...

'Have you had breakfast?'

'Not yet.'

'Then maybe we should go and do something about that.'

'I had pancakes yesterday. Mummy had a fig.'

'Wouldn't you like to try one?' He indicated the tree above them. 'You could pick your own if you like.'

The boy needed no second bidding, but leapt to his feet. Then, 'I can't, it's too high!'

'No problem,' Zahir said, picking him up, but, as he hoisted him to his shoulder, they both turned as they heard Diana making her way up the steps from the beach. She was singing slightly breathless snatches of lyrics from a familiar song, filling in the missing words with the odd 'la-la' as she had when they'd danced.

'La-la, la-la... La-la, la-la...'

She appeared on the path below them, for a moment totally unaware that she had an audience. Then, as Freddy giggled, she looked up, saw them together and stopped in mid 'la'...

And his mouth dried.

She had been for an early morning dip and was

wearing nothing but a simple one-piece bathing costume. Her creamy skin had dried on the walk up from the beach, but her hair was a mass of wet ringlets that dripped tiny rivulets of water on to her shoulders. Venus herself could not have been more beautiful, more enticing.

'Zahir…' She seemed as lost for words as he was. Then, recovering first, she said, 'I see you've met Freddy.'

'He's rather younger than I imagined…'

'I'm not young, I'm five!' the boy declared.

'But very big for five,' Zahir added quickly.

And Diana smiled.

Stood there in his garden, bare legs, bare shoulders, every curve of her body brought into the sharpest focus by the clinging fabric of her wet bathing suit, smiling that sweet, tender smile that would have tempted a saint. And he was no saint.

But then neither, it appeared, was she.

'I imagine he gets that from his father?' he prompted and her smile, along with the flush of exertion from the walk up from the beach, disappeared like water poured on sand.

'Freddy, I think we'd better go and find Grandma.' She extended her hand. 'Come on, she'll be wondering where we are.'

'I don't *think* so,' he said. Five years old and already resisting the tug of the apron strings.

'Freddy!'

'I *looked*. She's asleep.' The boy looked at him, a mute appeal for backup.

'Freddy and I were about to pick some figs. I'd invite you to join us but, much as I regret the fact, I'm afraid that with your colouring, you need to cover up before the sun gets any higher.'

Cover up…

Diana felt the heat flood into her cheeks as she realised just how little she was wearing. Just an old bathing suit that had been purchased for respectability rather than glamour. Something to wear when she took Freddy to mother and child swimming classes.

She hadn't even thought to take a towel with her, too locked into the idea of plunging into cold water to cool her overheated body.

Zahir was the last person she'd imagined meeting. Zahir looking at her as if she were Eve and it was the first morning…

'Um… Good plan…' she said, backing away in the direction of the house. 'You two g-go and make a start, while I…' she made a vague gesture to indicate her lack of covering, instantly regretting drawing further attention to the fact '…cover up.'

Then she turned and ran.

By the time she'd showered and gone through her entire wardrobe looking for something that would counteract the swimsuit look without looking as if she were hiding—cropped trousers, a long shirt with the sleeves rolled up—breakfast was well under way.

Zahir looked up, smiled, then continued talking to her father. Her mother passed her a cup of coffee without saying a word. Freddy looked up and said, 'Z'hir's taking Grandpa and me out on a boat. Do you want to come?'

She looked up, met Zahir's eyes and they were both remembering another day, another boat…

'My father keeps a small dhow here. For fishing. It's pretty basic.'

'Then I'll pass, thanks.'

'Do you want to talk about it?'

Diana and her mother were sitting on a rock above the beach, looking out over the water, watching the dhow set off down the creek.

'There's nothing to talk about,' she said, tossing a pebble into the water.

'I haven't seen you this…' she sought for the word. '…this *lost* since you were expecting Freddy.'

'That was different,' she said quickly. Then, when her mother just raised a brow, she shook her head. 'I can't explain it, but it's different, okay?'

'How different?'

But maybe not that different.

'It's easy to see how your sheikh might dazzle

you,' her mother said. 'Sweep you off your feet. He's a very good-looking man. And charming too—'

'No.' Then, 'Well, yes. Obviously.'

The difference was that Pete O'Hanlon had dazzled her with his danger. Had tempted her for no other reason than because he could. Because it amused him to take something untouched and mark it as his own. He did not build things, cherish things or people. He destroyed them...

Zahir was nothing like that.

Her mother looked anxious.

'He didn't dazzle me.' At least not intentionally.

All it had taken was one look and she'd lost it. All that painfully learned control, forgotten in an instant, gone in a look.

Okay. That was the same.

But she wasn't an eighteen-year-old with her hormones on fire. She'd kept it together for Freddy. Just...

She turned to her mother. 'How can one look change everything?' she asked, needing someone older, wiser to tell her. 'How can I feel this way about someone I met a couple of days ago?'

He'd looked at her as if she were the first woman and she hadn't wanted to run and hide. She'd wanted to touch him. Had wanted him to touch her.

That was different.

She'd made him laugh.

He'd made her want to dance. Made her feel brand-new…

'I don't know,' her mother replied. 'How do you feel?'

'As if…' As if he had been made just for her. 'As if he's a perfect fit,' she said. 'As if it's…*right.*'

And that was different too.

She'd known from the moment he'd taken what he wanted that everything about Pete O'Hanlon was wrong. That she'd been an idiot. That the next day he wouldn't even remember her name…

'It's a mystery. They say it's just chemical attraction. Sexual attraction is nature's way of keeping the species going. Marriage is society's way of dealing with the consequences.' She smiled. 'Or it was.' She shook her head, sighed. 'It doesn't explain how I knew your father was the one the minute he looked at me, though.' Then, smiling, 'Or maybe it does. Maybe it was no more than lust and I just got lucky.'

'It's more than that. You love each other.'

'It takes a lot of love to hold a marriage together for twenty-five years. Not that falling-in-love kind of love, though. It's the love you work at, that evolves, changes to match everything that life throws at the pair of you. But luck helps.'

When Diana didn't respond, she said, 'Maybe this is your time to get lucky. Does Zahir feel the same way about you?'

'It doesn't matter what he feels.' Her voice was more emphatic than her feelings.

That he was feeling something she never doubted. That he desired her. That if she'd been a different kind of woman, one who didn't have to live well one hundred per cent of the time just to make up for the one time she hadn't, they might have had a brief, exciting fling.

But that was all it could ever be.

'In this world, Zahir's world, marriages are arranged. He will marry someone his family, his peers, deem a perfect match.'

Her mother frowned. 'He told you that?'

'We were discussing fairy tales. It came up…'

'There's no room for romance?'

'Respect lasts longer,' she said, managing a smile for her mother. Wanting to reassure her that this time she wasn't going to fall apart. 'We both agreed that fairy tales are for children.'

'And meanwhile he can dance in the street with any girl who catches his eye?'

'Nothing happened. Truly. If it hadn't been for that photograph…'

If it hadn't been for that photograph they'd be back in their own little worlds. She'd be back on the school minibus. He'd be doing whatever billionaire sheikhs did. 'A couple of kisses, that idiotic dance…'

'Sometimes that's all it takes,' her mother said, laying a hand gently over hers. 'A look, a kiss, for the magic to change everything. How many men have you kissed? I mean kissed wanting more?'

'Only one.'

'Freddy's father?'

Diana looked out across the water. Could see Zahir and her father laughing at something Freddy had said or done. It was the perfect image. A little boy with two strong men to keep him safe. Except that Zahir would be gone in an hour or two and, once they'd left this beautiful place, their worlds would not touch again.

'No,' she said. 'Not Freddy's father.'

'Diana…'

She turned her hand to clasp her mother's fingers. She'd never told. She'd protected Freddy. Had protected her family. Had protected everyone except herself.

It was a secret that had stood between her and her parents for nearly six years. When she'd put up that wall of silence, had refused to confide in them, had refused to cave into the threats of the Child Support Agency, telling them what to do with their money, something had been lost…

'Don't ask, Mum. If you knew, you'd look at him differently. You wouldn't be able to help yourself.'

Instead of pressing her, her mother just squeezed

her hand. 'I'm proud of you, Diana. You're a strong woman and Freddy's a lucky boy…'

When the men returned, bearing their trophy fish, her mother took Freddy away to clean him up, her father went to take a nap, leaving her alone in the garden with Zahir.

'We have had no time to talk,' he said, 'and now I have to go.'

'Thank you for giving Freddy such a treat.'

'It was a pleasure. He's a lovely boy. But then he has a lovely mother. Walk with me to my car?'

She followed him up steps at the side of the house to a courtyard. It had been dark when they'd arrived, but now she could see that it commanded a view of the entire creek, and because she knew he was going to say something she didn't want to hear, she said, 'This is beautiful, Zahir. Has it always belonged to your family?'

'No. I came across the house when I was out sailing one weekend. A storm blew up and I took shelter in the creek. The place was uninhabited, falling to rack and ruin, but it was love at first sight and I bought it. Restored it.'

'You've done all this?'

'I made a start, did the early clearance, but life intruded. My family needed me. Then I got involved with the travel business. The truth of the matter is that these days I speak and it is done.'

'But the vision, the dream, is yours.'

'A man needs dreams to sustain him,' he said, turning abruptly away, opening the car door.

'We all need dreams.' Then, because the lie she had told hung between them and she wanted this over so that she could draw a line, begin to move on, she said, 'About Freddy…'

He stopped. 'You think that is why I came here today?' he said, not turning. 'To ask about your son?'

'Didn't you?' Then, when he didn't answer, 'I let you think he was my lover so that you would walk away.'

He straightened. 'Because you did not trust me.'

'No! Because I did not trust myself…'

As he swung round to face her, she faltered. 'Because once, when I was eighteen, I lost my head and hurt everyone who loved me…'

'Is being a single mother such a big deal these days?'

'No, but being a single mother and refusing to name the father is a very big deal.'

Zahir frowned. 'Why would you protect a man from his responsibilities?'

'I wasn't protecting him, I was protecting Freddy. I didn't want him tainted. Didn't want anyone to look at him and say, "Like father, like son…"

Always be looking for the first sign that he was going the same way.'

He reached out, caught her elbow, and somehow she was leaning against him, his arm around her, not in an embrace, but as support.

'I was supposed to be the level-headed one in my year. The daughter every mother wanted...' She gulped. 'Maybe that was part of it. I was tired of being good. I just wanted to be like everyone else, part of the gang, but all those boys at school were so...ordinary.'

'And it took extra-ordinary to make you bad?' he said gently.

'Pete O'Hanlon was different. Five years older. And so gloriously, perfectly dangerous.'

The words, his name, had spilled out before she was even aware she was thinking them. More than she'd told her mother. More than she'd told anyone.

'He was the worst nightmare of every woman with an impressionable daughter. And boy, was I impressionable? He'd moved away, no one knew where he'd gone, what he was doing, but his cousin was in the same class at school as me and he came to her eighteenth birthday party. The air buzzed when he walked in. Every girl was suddenly taller, more alive. Every boy looked...dull.'

'But he chose you...'

He'd waited until she was leaving. Had caught up with her, offered her a lift home.

'There are more dangerous things than walking home alone in the dark,' Zahir said when, finally, she stopped. 'Where is he now?'

'The morning after I got everything I deserved,' she said. 'He and three other men held up a bank. The police were waiting. He tried to shoot his way out and was killed.' She shuddered. 'I may be wrong, but I don't believe that Sadie Redford would be so quick to invite Freddy over for a play-date with her little girl if she knew that.'

'The sins of the father?'

The only sound was the air humming as the heat intensified. The high pitched note of cicadas stridulating below them in the garden. The blood pulsing in her ears as she waited for him to say something, anything.

'You are his mother, Diana. Nothing else matters.'

'No.' Then, shaking her head, 'Why did you come, Zahir?'

'Because…' He lifted his hand to her cheek. 'Because I could not stop myself.' He did not smile as he added, 'It seems that I am not as strong as you.'

For a moment she thought he would kiss her, but he let his hand fall to his side.

'You should get out of the sun now.' Then, as he climbed into the car, 'I promised Freddy that I would take him sailing tomorrow. I'll be here at six.'

* * *

Zahir walked with Shula al-Attiyah in his mother's garden, while their mothers gossiped and kept an eye on them. She was, just as his mother had promised, intelligent, well travelled, lively. Perfect in every respect but one. She was not Diana Metcalfe.

He sailed with Freddy the following morning and afterwards he ate a sumptuous *mezza* served by Hamid in the shade of the terrace with Diana and her family. Then he walked with Diana in the garden as he had walked with Shula.

He could not have said what they talked about. Only that being with her was right. That leaving her felt like tearing himself in half.

In the afternoon he met Adina al-Thani. She was the girl recommended by his sister for the beauty of her hair. It was a smooth ebony curtain of silk that hung to her waist and it was indeed beautiful.

If it had been chestnut. If curls had corkscrewed every which way, it would have been perfect.

Later, he had dinner with his father, who had just returned from the Sudan. They talked about politics. About the new airline. They did not talk about his marriage. Or the visitors occupying his house at Nadira.

But when he was leaving his father said, 'I want you to know that I'm proud of you, my son. This country needs men like you. Men who can take the future and mould it to their own vision.'

And he wasn't sure if that made him feel better, or worse.

The next day he was forced to remain in the capital, deal with the mountain of paperwork that was coming in from London. Have lunch with Leila al-Kassami—the one who was not beautiful but had a lovely smile—and her mother.

She, of all of them, came closest to his heart's desire. Perhaps if the smile had been preceded by the fleeting appearance of a dimple, if she had caught her lip between her teeth to stop herself from saying the first thing that came into her head...

As they left, he saw his mother watching him with an expression close to desperation and knew that he was running out of time.

That evening he took Diana on a tour of his 'vision'. Showed her the cottages, the central building that would provide everything a visitor could dream of. The chandlery, the marina. The island where the restaurant was nearing completion. The pavilion where people seeking somewhere different to hold a wedding could make their vows.

She stood beside him beneath the domed canopy looking up at the tiny lapis and gold tiles that looked like the sky in that moment before it went black and said, 'It's beautiful, Zahir.' And then she looked at him. 'Like something out of a fairy tale.'

'Wait until you see the real thing…'

'Oh, but I have…'

'No. Tonight I'll drive you far beyond the reach of man-made light—only there is it possible to see the heavens as God made them.'

Once darkness fell, he'd take her into the desert and, maybe, beneath the infinity of the heavens, she would be able to understand, he would be able to understand why, despite the fact that she had somehow taken possession of his heart, tomorrow he would have to redeem his promise to his mother. Do his duty as a son.

'I will not be able to come here again during your visit,' he said. 'But I want to give you this gift.'

Diana heard the words. Heard more, perhaps, than he'd intended to say. Something that they had both agreed upon from the very first. That there were no fairy tales.

CHAPTER ELEVEN

ZAHIR was unusually silent on the trip out into the desert but, when he stopped the big four-wheel drive, he told Diana to close her eyes before he killed the engine. Turned off the lights.

'Keep them closed,' he warned, as he opened the door, letting in a blast of cold air. She heard him walk around the vehicle, then he opened the door beside her.

'Here, take my cloak, you'll need it,' he said, dumping something heavy in her lap, before lifting her clear of her seat.

'Zahir!' she protested. 'I'm not helpless. I can walk!'

'Not if your eyes are closed.' Then, 'You might want to hold on.'

Obediently, she wrapped one arm around his neck, clutching the cloak to her with the other, while he carried her surely and safely over ground that crunched beneath his feet. Cheating a little, lifting her lids a fraction so that she could watch his face, the way his breath condensed in little clouds in the faint light from the stars.

'Can I look now?' she asked when he set her on her feet.

'I'll tell you when,' he said, taking the cloak and wrapping it around her. Then, standing behind her, his hands on either side of her shoulders as if afraid she might fall, he said, 'Now!'

She would have gasped if she could have caught her breath. Instead, soundlessly, she reached out, first to the sky, then back for his hand. As if he knew exactly how she would react, he was there, waiting for her, taking her hand in his.

How long they'd been standing there when the cold finally penetrated her brain, she could not have said.

'You must be freezing,' she said and, half turning, she opened the cloak, inviting him to share the warmth. When he hesitated, she said, 'Come on, before I freeze too.'

He joined her, slipping his arm around her waist to bring them close enough to fit in together and they stood, wrapped up in its warmth, for the longest time, her head on his shoulder, looking at the heavens. Diana knew, just knew, that this would be the moment she would remember when she was dying.

'I never dreamed,' she said at last, 'that there were so many stars.'

'They say that if you took a handful of sand from a beach and each grain of sand was a star you can see—'

'—the rest of the beach would represent the stars that are out of sight. I read that somewhere, but when you see it, really see it, it's…incomprehensible.'

'In the face of such vastness it is impossible not to feel…humble.'

'Yes,' she said. Then, lifting her head, turning to look at him, 'But how great too! We're standing here, looking up into the unimaginable vastness of space, and our imagination isn't crushed by that; it soars!'

In the starlight she could see a frown pucker in the space between his eyes.

'All through history we've looked up there and made stories, strived to know the unknowable. We're less than grains of sand in the cosmic scheme of things, no more than the tiniest particles of dust, and yet we're huge. Giants.' She turned and stretched her arms up to the stars. 'We're the star-gatherers, Zahir! We can do anything, be anyone. Only our own fears hold us back…' And she'd spent too many years afraid to step out of the shadows. Afraid to grab the world by the throat. Seize the dream. 'Thank you. Thank you for showing me that…'

And then, because one dream was all she had, because they both knew that this was goodbye, she leaned into him, kissed him briefly on the lips, before saying, 'I need to go home.'

When Diana called James Pierce it was still dark at Nadira. By the time her mother was awake, she had packed.

'Where are you going?'

'Home.' Her mother looked doubtful. 'It's okay. According to Mr Pierce, some supermodel had a furniture-throwing fight with her boyfriend in a nightclub and they both got arrested. Our little story can't begin to compete with that.'

'Well, that's good, but do you have to rush back to London? You're on leave, anyway.'

'There are things I have to do, but you're all staying until Saturday. Mr Pierce is sorting flights for you. Hamid will have all the details.'

'And Zahir?'

'He's been more than generous with his time, but he's got a business to run. He won't have time to come out here again.'

'I'm sorry.'

'No.' She blinked away the sting of a tear. No tears... 'No regrets.' She hugged her. 'Give Freddy a hug from me. See you at the weekend.'

And two hours after that she was on her way to London, this time flying business class on a scheduled flight.

She suspected James Pierce would have put her in economy if he'd dared and actually she didn't blame him. She'd messed up his boss's big week. Had made extra work for him.

The only thing they'd both agreed on was that Zahir should not be told until she was home. She'd scarcely expected to find James himself waiting to meet her, drive her home. A journey accomplished in almost total silence.

It was barely dark, just on nine, when he pulled up in front of Aunt Alice's. She didn't believe for a minute that anyone would be hanging around the house, but someone in the street would undoubtedly have taken the tabloid shilling to call in the moment she put in an appearance. She didn't blame them for that, but she wasn't prepared to make it easy for them either.

'Thank you, Mr Pierce. I'm very grateful—'

He dismissed her gratitude with a gesture. Then, 'I don't understand.' She waited. 'Why didn't you sell your story?'

'There is no story,' she said.

'When did that matter?'

She shook her head. 'I wouldn't do that to anyone, let alone someone I…' She stopped. 'Anyone.'

'No. I'm sorry, Miss Metcalfe. I saw how Zahir looked at you and feared exactly this, but I misjudged you. I thought you were—'

'A girl on the make?' She said it before he did.

'Under normal circumstances it wouldn't have mattered but Sheikh Zahir's family are in the middle of marriage negotiations on his behalf. It's a very bad moment to have some sordid story spread all over the media...'

'Arranged...' A small sound, as if all the breath had been driven from her, escaped Diana before she could stop it. 'Now?'

That was why he'd whisked her and her family to Nadira? Not concern for her, as she'd thought, but to keep her isolated? Out of the clutches of the press until the fuss had died down?

'It's the way they do things,' James said, mistaking her reaction for shock. Why would she be shocked? He'd told her how they did things...

But while she'd unburdened herself, had spilled out the secret she hadn't even shared with her mother, he had kept this from her.

'If there's anything you need,' James continued, clearly anxious to be on his way. 'If you have any problems, please give me a call.' He handed her a card. 'I'll be staying in London for the foreseeable future.' He gave the smallest of shrugs and said, 'Zahir appointed me CEO of the airline before he left.'

She remembered. He'd mentioned it when they'd been at the yacht club. 'Congratulations.' Then, pulling herself together, trying to hang on to her sudden elation as she'd looked up at the stars, 'Maybe there is something. I'm going to need a bank loan to buy my first taxi. The last time I tried, I was shown the door.'

'You want to buy a taxi? Don't you have to pass tests to get a licence to drive a London cab?'

'I was nearly there once.' Then her dad had a stroke and her life had hit the skids for the second time and it had felt like punishment for her sins… 'I can do it again.'

'Oh, well, under the circumstances I'm sure Sheikh Zahir would be more than willing to—'

'No!' Then, 'No. That's not what I'm asking for. I don't want his money. Not even as a loan. What I want is for the bank manager to treat me with respect. Take me seriously.'

'I see. Well, in that case you're going to need a business plan and an accountant.' And wonder of wonders, he smiled. 'In fact you might try the Prince's Trust. They help young people set up in business. I'll make some enquiries.'

'No…'

She wasn't crawling back into her rut. She'd allowed herself to love someone and the world hadn't fallen apart. She'd seen the universe and she'd been inspired.

'Thank you, James, but I can do that.'

'I don't doubt it, Miss Metcalfe, but the number on the card is a direct line to my office. Give me a call if I can help.'

Zahir found his mother sitting in her garden. Kissed her cheek, took her hand.

'Are you well?' he asked, sitting beside her.

'By the will of Allah,' she said. 'And you, Zahir?'

'By the will of Allah,' he replied.

She smiled up at him. 'You look happy. I can see that you have made your decision.'

'I have. It was not easy but the woman who has won my heart has warmth, sweetness, honour. She has courage too. And family is everything to her.'

'Then it seems that I have found you a paragon!'

'No man could...' or would, he thought '...live with a paragon. Except my father,' he added swiftly. 'The women you chose were all equally charming and any one of them would make a perfect wife. For someone else.'

Her smile faded. 'Zahir...'

'When I was young, I had Hanif to speak for me, talk to my father, persuade him to let me take my own path, even though it was not the one chosen for me. Have I failed you, have I brought dishonour on my family?'

'My son...' She shook her head. Laid a hand over his.

'Now I am a man and I must speak for myself. I honour you and my father, as I have always honoured you. Will you not trust me in this greatest of all decisions to know my own heart?'

Alone in the house, Diana hadn't put the light on but had curled up in bed, hugging the cat for comfort.

She'd woken early—she'd just about adjusted to Ramal Hamrah time—and, because the alternative was lying there thinking about Zahir standing under that canopy with some perfect match his family had found for him, she got up and set about making a plan.

No. Not the canopy. He'd said that traditional weddings took place in the bride's home. Well, obviously, he'd been thinking about it...

She concentrated on the list of things to do. First thing she'd call the Public Carriage Office and talk to someone about getting back on track with her 'appearances'—the tests of her knowledge of the quickest routes in London.

Then she'd go to the library and use the computer to follow up the stuff James Pierce had mentioned, check on the possibility of a start-up grant.

A princess.

She'd bet they'd found him a princess to marry.

Well, that was how it was in real life. Princes married princesses while Cinderella…got the frog.

She called Sadie.

'It's quiet here. No one at Capitol is prepared to talk and the media was reduced to printing a fuzzy school photograph of you.'

'Oh, terrific. One minute I'm hanging off the arm of a sheikh in the hat from hell, the next the world sees me in pigtails!'

'You looked cute.'

'I'm twenty-three. Cute is not a good look!' Then, 'I just hope that whoever sold it to them made them pay through the nose.'

She got a couple of startled looks from the neighbours as she walked down the street, but she just smiled and said, 'Gorgeous day!' and walked on. Called in at the bank to make an appointment. Visited the library.

She thought she was home clear when a journalist caught up with her in the supermarket.

'Nice tan, Diana. Been somewhere nice?'

'Do I know you?'

'Jack Harding. *The Courier.* Ramal Hamrah is very nice at this time of year, I believe.'

'And you would know that how?' she asked.

It was surreal but she refused to duck and run. She would not hide. Instead, she carried on shopping, bought cheese, eggs, apples.

By the time she reached the checkout there were three of them.

'Will you be seeing the Sheikh again?'

'Can you pass me down that jar of tomato paste.' she replied.

'Are you going back to work?'

'Haven't you lot got a supermodel to harass?' she asked, losing patience.

'She's in rehab. And Cinderella is a much better story.'

'It's a fairy tale,' she replied. Then, 'Are you lot going to follow me home?'

'Will you make us a cup of tea and tell us your life story if we do?'

'No, but you could make yourself useful,' she said, pointing at her shopping. 'Carry that.' She didn't wait to see whether any of them picked up her bags, but just walked out.

She let them follow her up to the front door before she retrieved the carriers with a smile. 'Thank you.' Then, as she slipped the key into the lock, she glanced back. 'Will you be here tomorrow?'

'What's happening tomorrow?'

'Nothing. But the grass needs cutting and because of you lot Dad isn't here to do it.'

They laughed, but with the embarrassment of men who'd been caught out misbehaving.

'No? Well, sorry guys, but that's as exciting as it's

going to get around here.' And with that she stepped inside, closed the door on them and leaned back against it, shaking like a leaf. So much for it all being over.

But she'd survived. And as soon as they realised there really was nothing in it for them, they'd drift away. A week from now no one would even remember that she'd danced with a sheikh in Berkeley Square.

Well, except for whoever made a little cash selling an old school photograph.

And her.

Her fairy tale prince might be unattainable, but he was unforgettable. And he had made the magic happen, had brought the world into focus, had reminded her that dreaming was allowed. That anyone could do it. That she could do anything...

Next year she'd have her own taxi. A pink, sparkly one that would turn heads, make people smile. And every day when she drove it around London, she'd thank him for hauling her out of the deep rut she had been digging for herself, had been hiding in.

She drew in a deep breath and walked through to the kitchen. Dumped her bags on the table.

The cat rubbed against her leg, then crossed to the door and, refusing to submit to the indignity of the cat flap when there was a human on hand to open the door, waited to be let out.

'You are such a princess,' Diana said, opening the

door with a mock curtsey. And found herself staring at her fantasy.

The desert prince she had expected when she'd dashed to the City Airport. The whole white robes, gold-trimmed cloak, headdress thingy.

But it wasn't his robes that held her. She'd recognised what he was even in the most casual clothes. Now, as then, it was Zahir's dark eyes that drained the power of speech as she relived that moment when she'd first set eyes on him. But this time she recognised it for what it was.

The prelude to pain…

Ten minutes ago her life had seemed so simple. Her sights fixed on an attainable goal. Her heart safely back behind locked doors.

Now…

'Your Aunt Alice was kind enough to let me come through her garden,' he said, answering the what-the-hell-are-you-doing-here? question she'd been unable to frame. He shrugged. Smiled. Just with his eyes.

Oh, no…

'Aunt Alice!' she exploded. 'Why did you bother coming in the back way if you're going to come dressed like Lawrence of…' she struggled to keep the expletive in check '…of Arabia?' She made a wild gesture that took in his clothes. 'And where did you park your camel?'

'I hate to disappoint you, Diana, but I came by cab.'

'Oh, great! The driver is probably calling in the story right now. I've only just got rid of three journalists who followed me home…'

And, grabbing his arm, she pulled him into the kitchen, shut the door and leaned back against it, hands pressed to her lips.

'It was not my intention to sneak in unobserved, but I only had Aunt Alice's address.' Then, taking her hands from her mouth, kissing each of them, he said, 'I suppose I could have walked along this street knocking on doors until I found you—'

'You might as well have done!'

Then, with a gesture of helplessness, she let it go. What mattered was not how but *why* he'd come.

'What are you doing here, Zahir?' she demanded. 'I've just about got my head around this and you've chosen to turn a nine-day wonder into a front page story…'

'I have nothing to hide and neither have you.' Then, 'Freddy asked me to give you this.' From somewhere in the folds of his robe he produced a small piece of rope. 'He wanted you to see the reef knot we made.'

Diana took it. It was warm and without thinking, she lifted it to her cheek.

Then, looking up at him, 'We?'

'The two of us.'

'But… You said you wouldn't be going back to Nadira this week.'

'Is that why you left?'

'No…' Then, because he deserved better than some feeble lie, 'Maybe. But it was more than that. You listened to my story and you…' She reached for the words. 'You set me free, Zahir. Showed me how insignificant we are, but how great too. I've spent years expecting nothing. Believing that I was worth nothing—'

'Believing that you were the frog?' He smiled. 'Don't you know that once you've been kissed by a prince all bets are off?'

'No. The true meaning of the fairy story is that we are all princesses. It's just that some of us lose the ability to see that. But you treated me like one. Gave me the courage to believe. To gather my own stars.'

There was a long peal on the doorbell. It hadn't taken long…

'Speaking of fairy stories, why did you come back, Zahir? Haven't you got something more important to do? Like arranging your marriage?'

Far from looking like a man caught out, he said, 'That's the beauty of a system like ours, Diana. Once I have made my decision, chosen my bride, I don't have to do a thing. Even as we speak, my mother is negotiating with my bride's family, drawing up the contract.'

'I can't believe you're saying that. It's…gruesome.'

'No, no… I promise you, the women will have a very happy time disposing of my assets. Squabbling over the exact size of the house my bride is to have in London—'

'A house?'

In London?

'A woman must have a house of her own. Suitably furnished, of course. An income to maintain it. A car.' He considered that. 'Make that two.'

'For heaven's sake!'

Tiny lines creased around his eyes in the prelude to a smile. 'Princesses are high maintenance.' There was another long peal on the doorbell, followed by an insistent knock. 'Do you want to get that?'

'No, thanks.'

He continued to look at her. 'Where was I?'

'High maintenance,' she managed. 'Two cars.'

'Oh, yes. Then, once all the practical stuff is out of the way, they get to the really good stuff. The jewels I will give her…'

She clutched her arms tightly around her waist, trying to hold herself together, and, as if to ease her pain, he laid his hand against her cheek, so that without meaning to she was looking up at him.

'My mother thinks I should give her diamonds, but I disagree. I think nothing would become her throat more than the soft lustre of pearls…'

'Please, Zahir! Don't do this to me.'

'What, *ya malekat galbi*? What, the owner of my heart, am I doing to you?'

'You know.' She moaned as, trapped, she had nowhere to run. No escape from his touch, from her body's urgent response to the darkening of his eyes, his scent…

'Tell me.'

'I can't be what you want me to be. Maybe an arranged marriage is different. Maybe with her house, income, jewels, your wife won't care whether you are faithful or not. But I do. I can't, I won't be your mistress!'

Even to her own ears, her cry had sounded desperate and he took her hand from her waist, lifting it to lay it over his heart, with the words, '*Ya rohi, ya hahati*. My soul, my life… I believe you.' And, as if to prove her a liar, her knees buckled and she fell into his waiting arms.

'Please,' she begged, her face pressed against his chest so that she could feel the steady, powerful beat of his heart. But what she was begging for, release or thrall, she no longer knew or cared.

He gathered her in and held her for a moment, his arms around her, his cheek resting against her head. And for a moment she felt as if she was in the safest place in the world and she cared. Cared more than anything. That gave her the strength to pull away.

For a moment he resisted, then he kissed the top of her head, eased her into the battered armchair which, since his stroke, her father used when her mother was busy in the kitchen—so that they could be together, talk, as she did the ironing, baked. It seemed to symbolise everything that was good and true and pure about their long marriage.

Everything that she was not…

As she made to move, get up, Zahir stopped her, knelt at her feet. 'Maybe just one diamond,' he said. And, opening his palm, he revealed an antique ring, a large emerald cut diamond supported by emeralds. 'A pledge, my promise, while your mother and mine enjoy themselves squabbling over where your house will be—in Mayfair or Belgravia—whether you should have diamonds or pearls, or both. Arranging our marriage.' He slipped the ring on to her finger. Kissed the backs of her fingers, kissed her palm. 'The beauty of a system like *yours*, twin of my soul, is that I do not have to wait until the contract is signed before I may see you. Talk with you. Be alone with you. Kiss you…'

His kiss was long, lingering, sweet…

The doorbell rang again. Someone hammered on the back door. Then the telephone started ringing.

Zahir drew back.

'That would be alone with a media circus…'

'Well, what on earth were you thinking? If you'd worn jeans, you might have got away with it.'

'When a man asks a woman to be his wife, jeans will not do.' Then, 'Shall we make their day and go outside, pose for photographs? You can show them your ring, have your own Princess Diana moment.'

'I don't think so! Not until I've done my hair. Changed into something to match my prince.' She drew back, shook her head. 'How can I do this? I'm no princess.'

'Believe me, you're a natural, but if you are concerned about how we will live, your life, talk to Lucy. When she tells you her story, you'll understand that anything is possible.'

'Really?'

'Remember the stars.'

'And Freddy?'

'Freddy is your son and when we are married he will be mine, Diana. Ours,' he said, thumbing a tear from her cheek. 'Frederick Trueman Metcalfe bin Zahir al-Khatib. The first of our children.'

'I need to learn Arabic, Zahir. Will you teach me?'

They had stopped on their way from the airport to walk in the desert. A last moment alone before they were plunged into wedding celebrations. To look again at the stars.

He turned to her and she leaned into him for his

warmth, for him to hold her. Wrapping his arms around her, he said, 'Where do you want to start?'

'*Sitti*,' she said. 'Hamid calls me *sitti*. What does it mean?'

'Lady.'

'*Lady*? Goodness.' Then, 'And Lord?'

'*Sidi*.'

'Tell me more, *sidi*,' she said, smiling up at him. 'What is *ya habibati*?'

'You have a good ear for the sound, my beloved. But a woman, if she called her husband "my beloved" would say *ya habibi*.'

'Tell me more, *sidi, ya habibi*.'

'To a child, to Freddy, I would say *ya rohi, ya hahati*. My soul, my life.'

She repeated the words. 'That's beautiful, but you might be better not telling him what it means.'

'He is beautiful. You are beautiful, *ya malekat galbi*. The owner of my heart. *Ahebbak, ya tao'am rohi*.' Then, after a slow, searing kiss that heated her body, melted her heart with his love, 'I love you, the twin of my soul.'

'*Ahebbak*, Zahir. I love you.' Then, as they walked on, 'I think I'm going to enjoy learning Arabic.'

He stopped. 'There is one more phrase I must teach you, *ya rohi. Amoot feeki*. There is no life without you, Diana.'

She took his hands, raised them to her lips. '*Amoot feeki*, Zahir. Is that right?'

He smiled. 'As good as it gets.' Then, 'It's nearly dawn. 'Come. I have something for you.'

'What? What more could I possibly want, dream of? A house in Belgravia, a BMW, more pearls than the ocean. Diamonds like the stars…'

'This is not something to be written down. This is a gift of the heart. My promise that I will always, before anything, do all I can to make your dreams come true.'

'Zahir… Every dream, every possible dream…'

'Shh… Wait…'

Dawn was turning the sky pink and blue as they reached Nadira and, as they drove in through the gates, the sun burst above the horizon to light up a pink, sparkly Metro taxi.

* * * * *

Love Inspired
HISTORICAL

*Powerful, engaging stories of romance,
adventure and faith
set in the past—when life was simpler and faith
played a major role in everyday lives.*

Turn the page for a sneak preview of
THE BRITON
by
Catherine Palmer

*Love Inspired Historical—love and faith
throughout the ages
A brand-new line from Steeple Hill Books
Launching this February!*

"Welcome to the family, Briton," said one of Olaf's men in a mocking voice. "We look forward to the presence of a woman at our hall."

Bronwen grasped her tunic and yanked it from the Viking's thick fingers. As she stepped away from the table, she heard the drunken laughter of the barbarians behind her. How could her father have betrothed her to the old Viking?

Running down the stone steps toward the heavy oak door that led outside from the keep, Bronwen gathered her mantle about her. She ordered the doorman to open the door, and he did so reluctantly, pressing her to carry a torch. But Bronwen pushed past him and fled into the darkness.

Dashing down the steep, pebbled hill toward the beach, she felt the frozen ground give way to sand. She threw off her veil and circlet and kicked away her shoes.

Racing alongside the pounding surf, she felt hot tears of anger and shame well up and stream down her cheeks. With no concern for her safety, Bronwen ran and ran—her long braids streaming behind her, falling loose, drifting like a tattered black flag.

Blinded with weeping, she did not see the dark form that sprang up in her path and stopped dead her headlong sprint. Bronwen shrieked in surprise and fear as iron arms pinned her, and a heavy cloak threatened to suffocate her.

"Release me!" she cried. "Guard! Guard, help me."

"Hush, my lady." A deep voice emanated from the darkness. "I mean you no harm. What demon drives you to run through the night without fear for your safety?"

"Release me, villain! I am the daughter—"

"I shall hold you until you calm yourself. We had heard there were witches in Amounderness, but I had not thought to meet one so openly."

Still held tight in the man's arms, Bronwen drew back and peered up at the hooded figure. "You! You are the man who spied on our feast. Release me at once, or I shall call the guard upon you."

The man chuckled at this and turned toward his companions, who stood in a group nearby. Bronwen caught hold of the back of his hood and jerked it down to reveal a head of glossy raven curls. But the man's face was shrouded in darkness yet, and as he looked at her, she could not read his expression.

"So you are the blessed bride-to-be." He returned the hood to his head. "Your father has paired you with an interesting choice."

Relieved that her captor did not appear to be a highwayman, she pushed away from him and sagged onto the wet sand. "Please leave me here alone. I need peace to think. Go on your way."

The tall stranger shrugged off his outer mantle and wrapped it around her shoulders. "Why did your father betroth you thus to the aged Viking?" he asked.

"For one purported to be a spy, you know precious little about Amounderness. But I shall tell you, as it is all common knowledge."

She pulled the cloak tightly about her, reveling in its warmth. "This land, known as Amounderness, once was Briton territory. Olaf Lothbrok, my betrothed, came here as a youth when the Viking invasions had nearly subsided. He took the lands directly to the south of Rossall Hall from their Briton lord. Then, of course, the Normans came, and Amounderness was pillaged by William the Conqueror's army."

The man squatted on the sand beside Bronwen. He listened with obvious interest as she continued. "When William took an account of Amounderness in his Domesday Book, he recorded no remaining lords and few people at all. But he did not know the Britons. Slowly we crept out of hiding and returned to our halls. My father's family reoccupied Rossall Hall. And there we live, as we should, watching over our serfs as they fish and grow their meager crops. Indeed, there is not much here for the greedy Normans to want, if they are the ones for whom you spy."

Unwilling to continue speaking when her heart was so heavy, Bronwen stood and turned toward the sea. The traveler rose beside her and touched her arm. "Olaf Lothbrok's lands—together with your father's—will reunite most of Amounderness under the rule of the son you are beholden to bear. A clever plan. Your sister's future husband holds the rest of the adjoining lands, I understand."

"You've done your work, sir. Your lord will be pleased. Who is he—some land-hungry Scottish baron? Or have you forgotten that King Stephen gave Amounderness to the Scots, as a trade for their support in his war with Matilda? I certainly hope your lord is not a Norman. He would be so disappointed to learn he has no legal rights here. Now, if you will excuse me?"

Bronwen turned and began walking back along the beach toward Rossall Hall. She felt better for her run, and somehow her father's plan did not seem so farfetched anymore. Distant lights twinkled through the fog that was rolling in from the west, and she suddenly realized what a long way she had come.

"My lady," the man's voice called out behind her.

Bronwen kept walking, unwilling to face again the one who had seen her in her humiliation. She didn't care what he reported to his master.

"My lady, you have quite a walk ahead of you." The traveler strode forward to join her. "I shall accompany you to your destination."

"You leave me no choice, I see."

"I am not one to compromise myself, dear lady. I follow the path God has set before me and none other."

"And just who are you?"

"I am called Jacques."

"French. A Norman, as I had suspected."

The man chuckled. "Not nearly as Norman as you are Briton."

As they approached the fortress, Bronwen could see that the guests had not yet begun to disperse. Perhaps no one had missed her, and she could slip quietly into bed beside Gildan.

She turned to go, but he took her arm and studied her face in the moonlight. Then, gently, he drew her into the folds of his hooded cloak. "Perhaps the bride would like the memory of a younger man's embrace to warm her," he whispered.

Astonished, Bronwen attempted to remove his arms from around her waist. But she could not escape his lips as they found her own. The kiss was soft and warm, melting away her resistance like the sun upon the snow. Before she had time to react, he was striding back down the beach.

Bronwen stood stunned for a moment, clutching his woolen mantle about her. Suddenly she cried out, "Wait, Jacques! Your mantle!"

The dark one turned to her. "Keep it for now," he shouted into the wind. "I shall ask for it when we meet again."

* * * * *

Don't miss this deeply moving story,
THE BRITON,
available February 2008
from the new Love Inspired Historical line.

And also look for
HOMESPUN BRIDE
by Jillian Hart,
where a Montana woman discovers that love
is the greatest blessing of all.

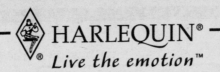

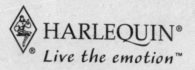

HARLEQUIN®
INTRIGUE®

BREATHTAKING ROMANTIC SUSPENSE

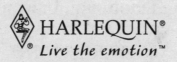

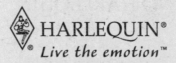

HARLEQUIN®
Presents

**The world's bestselling romance series...
The series that brings you your favorite authors,
month after month:**

Helen Bianchin...Emma Darcy
Lynne Graham...Penny Jordan
Miranda Lee...Sandra Marton
Anne Mather...Carole Mortimer
Susan Napier...Michelle Reid

and many more uniquely talented authors!

Wealthy, powerful, gorgeous men...
Women who have feelings just like your own...
The stories you love, set in exotic, glamorous locations...

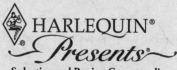

HARLEQUIN®
Presents

Seduction and Passion Guaranteed!

Harlequin® Historical
Historical Romantic Adventure!

*Imagine a time of chivalrous
knights and unconventional ladies,
roguish rakes and impetuous
heiresses, rugged cowboys
and spirited frontierswomen—
these rich and vivid tales will
capture your imagination!*

*Harlequin Historical...
they're too good to miss!*